PLAYA CRUSH

Ian Ostroff

CANADA

Cover Design by TWJ Design
ISBN (Paperback): 978-1-7781384-2-3
ISBN (Digital): 978-1-7781384-3-0

Dedication

To all those who struggled during the pandemic and got through it stronger.

PART 1:

A NEW LOST GENERATION

Chapter 1

March 25, 2022

There I was, half-drunk and walking along the nightlife district of Playa Del Carmen. From Calle 8 to every other corner of the tourist strip, another Friday night was beginning to come alive before my eyes. People from Europe, South America, the US, Canada, and other parts of Mexico filled Playa with the anticipation to dance for hours. Everyone around me was looking for an escape from the restrictions and darkness the pandemic brought to the world. There was an excitement in the air, knowing good vibes, positive energy, and a sense of life could be found in Playa—whether it was for one week or three months. I spotted attractive men tanning on the beach earlier that I wanted to befriend. There were beautiful women I wanted to spark a conversation with to see if I liked what was in their hearts. But instead of socializing, I continued to walk. That happened a lot ever since the first wave of COVID-19 broke out in March 2020.

All the long walks I took in the past two years, the movement of my feet, the exercise, and the daydreams I'd get of different planets and galaxies from the stars above kept me alive. I strolled around my old neighborhood in Montreal, not because I had no place to go, but because the circumstances only gave me this freedom. But now in Mexico, my world is not the same as it was back home. It's crazy how far I've come for nostalgia and human connection.

My name is Max Velasco. And believe it or not, this is what my life was like before the pandemic changed everything. I graduated from Concordia University in December 2020 with a bachelor's degree in journalism. I lived in a cheap, rundown apartment off Rene-Levesque and held the unfulfilled promises of "life after graduation" in my head. I wrote for my school paper and did everything right, yet it wasn't enough in the job market. I'd apply for a writing position on *LinkedIn* or *Indeed*, interview with companies that seemed to like me, make it past a couple of rounds and then get a depressing rejection email. It sucked to realize my name was one of maybe fifty others they were considering—my university peers and friends were my competition.

Looking back, history will probably say that I got into the job market at the worst time. It might be defined as a bad time for any young person in the 21st century to navigate the real world. But I still prayed to God—asking what my "next move" should have been. I hoped I'd get an office job somewhere, doing work that mattered, and surrounded by like-minded people with similar goals. Nowadays, it seemed like a dream of the past with all the remote positions out there. Home was the new "office", the new work environment, the new place to do everything. I was isolated from my friends, rarely saw family, and hated the fact my "co-workers" would be replaced by neighbors arguing over petty bullshit. But although it didn't look good, I tried to ignore the rumors of COVID-19. It might be sad, yet I recall hoping 2021 would be my "year".

After circling back to my hostel off *Calle 4*, I realized it was my unhealthy, toxic hustle culture mindset that motivated me to look for "job opportunities" after graduation. I filled out numerous applications and updated my resume daily, yet nobody ever gave me a break. Apparently, I didn't have the experience or connections to work in journalism, or anything, for that matter. College sent me out into the real world and expected me to leverage my expensive piece of paper only to be met by fake politeness at interviews, rejection, tears, and COVID-19.

But as I walked past a rooftop bar I've partied at many times, I knew the pandemic was creating a new lost generation of people in Mexico like the one in 1920s Paris, yet instead of writers and artists, there were digital nomads from a variety of fields. Speaking of which, I heard the Dutch friends I met back in Tulum call me from the rooftop balcony to join them. Happily, I cried out to them, "Yes, but just let me change out of my bathing suit first." They laughed. I also bumped into my Argentinian friends as they were on their way to Santino's—another club I frequented at Playa. *"Voy a estar allá luego en la noche,"* I said to them so they'd leave me alone. I kept on meeting pretty faces I encountered on the way back to my hostel for some reason. And that's when I thought of Milo—the DJ, my ex-best friend, and my first gay lover.

Life was simpler back then, and so were we. I remember our soccer playing days in high school, the lunch periods we shared, the jokes we had, the goals we scored, and the music we listened to together. I remember the week before prom when it was just us in the locker room. But I especially remember Milo telling me about his secrets and dreams—thoughts that meant nothing to me at the time yet have now led to this beautiful adventure in Mexico I'll never forget.

I learned Milo and I weren't the same people we once were at seventeen. Mentally and spiritually, the pandemic gave us a twisted sense of reality that caused this delusion. I knew that our relationship wouldn't ever last. Milo, on the other hand, thought we'd be in Mexico forever.

Each of us reflected different waves that crashed into La Riviera Maya. I was a small one that caused no alarms. But Milo was a monster that forced people to notice its picturesque image of nature. He was meant for great things since I met him at soccer tryouts during our freshman year of high school. Fast forward to 2022, I had maybe 1400 Instagram followers, and only enough money to rent a studio apartment. Milo was living in penthouses with access to private yachts he'd use for Instagram reels, TikTok, pics, and content to add to his 5.6 million followers.

But with that in mind, I caught up with my Argentinian friends to party it up at Santino's—kicking the sudden depression aside. Quietly, I ignored the problems in my life, the inevitable reason for the events that played out. It's hard to describe, but I needed to for Bellita.

This is where my story begins.

Chapter 2

February 15, 2021

Never was I the greatest student. It's an academic fate that stuck by my side dating back to elementary school. But there was something about becoming a journalist that captivated my heart. Even though I questioned my major every other week until graduating in December 2020, a part of me thought I was doing something useful. I was studying to be an important voice in my community, a public figure with news to share; a reliable personality to keep my fellow Montrealers in the know. I loved the responsibility of that kind of position. It's something I chased relentlessly in the job market. My dream was to be a storyteller. But after eight months of interviews and writing blogs for pocket money, my "career" remained stagnant.

Looking back, February 2021 was a hard time for every Montreal resident—especially since we were a month into an 8:00 p.m. curfew that seemed like it would last forever. The days were short, and hope was impossible to find. Even the news wasn't reliable anymore with the darkness it encouraged and its pointless clickbait. Maybe I was just another unemployed university graduate let down by a system that promised so much for the amount of tuition I paid, and the hours sacrificed to prepare for exams. Maybe it took a global pandemic to slow everything down to revaluate my life. I felt lonely and nostalgic as I sat with my laptop in my little apartment collecting the *CERB*—unable to invite guests over to hang out like in previous years. That's when I thought of what inspired me to believe that being a journalist was worth the struggle.

Out of every school assignment, I usually received a B average, with the occasional C or A- grade in between. Respectable, yet nothing compared to the inspired minds I met from Concordia and McGill. Doubts materialized about being a news anchor, a digital reporter, or even a staff writer at an online publication since I knew my competition. But as I reflect, there was one article that changed my life and perspective on my talent—my first end-of-semester feature article piece. It feels like it was a million years ago with the way COVID-19 lockdowns altered the perception of time. But I still recall how much fun I had on that assignment. I decided to do it on local DJs in Montreal—the ones who made nightclubs and bar scenes come alive on the weekend and during the summer months. I talked to veterans in the industry and absorbed a lot from it. But I also talked to my old high school friend Milo Dumont, a man I hadn't been in contact with since my seventeenth birthday years ago. It was a reunion that was long overdue.

Milo was not only my soccer teammate and best friend since Grade 7, but he was also the first person who knew I was bisexual. I loved him because of his big heart, his sense of humor, and the way I felt whenever I hung out with him alone. But as I found out a year after high school ended, I was also the first person who knew he was gay. Milo came from a religious Catholic family in Quebec, which always made him feel petrified to live out his authentic truth.

The difference between us was simple, though: I was attracted to feelings, the little things about a man or woman that made them special. But to avoid judgement, I hid my gay side from my family. I was a genuine coward, yet I also didn't want to deal with their reaction. All I needed to do was hook up with men without strings attached to keep up this secret. Looking back now, it's the reason why I'd lean toward the woman in my life who showed me interest. It was my way of proving to everyone around me that I was normal—even though I knew that was a lie.

But Milo struggled to hide his identity throughout his youth and finally shared that part of himself with his family when he turned eighteen. Around the time I reconnected with Milo for my article, he hadn't spoken to his parents in years. He worked at a fast-food joint by day and followed his DJ dreams at night —barely making enough to pay his rent. But even then, Milo was happy since he was pursuing something he loved. It was this passion for his craft that led to the only A+ grade I ever received. Even my teachers encouraged me to submit it to the university paper. It became a hit among my peers. I felt like a respected journalist in that brief moment.

Milo discussed the shows he did, the club owners who refused to pay him, the adrenaline rush when playing a set, and living his "ultimate dream" as a starving artist. It was a stereotype and a tragic love story that he was proud to own. And it was the rawness in Milo that my peers seemed to appreciate. They even asked me to do a follow-up. People started going to his shows because of that little 500-word assignment.

On that late February night after 8:00 p.m., something inside me wanted to pull out that old piece from a drawer in my bedroom. I kept the newspaper clipping, yet never got around to framing it. The first thing that surprised me was the date— February 18th, 2017. We were nearing the fourth anniversary. I still remember how I prayed Milo would find some direction back then. Passion and love could only get one so far. It was a reality Milo was aware of, too. But he was a dreamer if I've ever met one—a naïve, sensitive kid that escaped real life during our interview.

"I really just want people to dance and enjoy themselves when I play my sets," Milo said, as we hung out at a rundown bar off Crescent. "Maybe I'm broke now, but I know I won't be for long. I have ideas I've been working on and it's just a matter of time until I can afford the software to bring everything together. This new album I'm working on could actually be the difference between me playing ghetto clubs with asshole owners and playing major festivals."

The way Milo's eyes lit up was hard to ignore. Even though he dressed like a poor hipster and couldn't even afford the Heineken he drank, my friend was able to convince me it might all work out. And then, Milo went more in-depth and reached for my hand. Suddenly, butterflies rushed through me as if I was a teenager again. It was enough to ask more about his "goals."

"Good EDM music is about capturing feelings and sensations that words can never describe," Milo said when I asked him to explain the concept behind his album. "It has to be romantic, yet it also has to make you dance even if you can't. The music needs to resonate from the second it blasts from my USB to the speakers. And it also needs to leave you with a hangover, almost a depressive feeling when it's over. See, like... if you ask me, there are too many people out there who don't know how to express themselves. Maybe they really just need someone to understand they're not going through it alone. So, that's the concept: it's about life and hopelessness, but also about the beauty of letting go. It's going to explode, brother, I'm telling you. Remember this interview and keep this article somewhere when it comes out. I'm going to be a celebrity before I'm twenty-five. And you will be able to say you knew me first."

After that, we headed to his apartment building in Le Plateau. We drank a few more beers and reminisced about "us". Eventually, we made love in his bedroom before his roommates got home. Old feelings surfaced in both our hearts until we couldn't take it anymore. But the weirdest part was this: I was fresh out of a committed relationship with a girl in my program back then, yet never felt alive with her like I did at that moment. It took a one-night stand with Milo in 2017 to feel disgusted with the romantic side of my personality I wasn't able to control. It petrified me of what my family would've thought. Besides, they were almost sure I'd propose.

"So, would you like to come to my show next week?" Milo asked while I got dressed to leave. "I can put you on the guest list. Maybe you can film me doing my thing and you can attach it to your feature or whatever. I don't know, I feel it will probably show you can go the extra—"

"I don't think that'll be necessary!" I said, cutting him off. "Sorry... it's just this is only supposed to be a writing assignment, so I can't. But maybe next time! I'll have other projects."

"Okay, that's cool," Milo said after a long pause. "But can I at least show you a sample of what you'll be missing out on? You'll be the first to hear it, and it'll mean a lot. I love you, brother. And I know that I always will, no matter what happens. So... can you please hold on?"

Milo rushed to his desk once I nodded. It was as though he believed that his music would be powerful enough to make me want to stay. But I couldn't take that kind of risk—not when I was searching for a new girlfriend and had what I thought was a meaningful journalism career to pursue. I was doing everything "right" and Milo was a high school friend I outgrew. Before Milo played his sample, I mentioned I needed to get his article written, since it was fresh in my mind. Looking back, I knew Milo was devastated. In fact, he was on the verge of crying. I kissed Milo goodbye and said I'd be in touch. But once the article was submitted, I never saw him again.

Suddenly, I felt myself teleporting back to 2017 when I reread the piece. Every line made me reflect deeper on the interview we did, the natural flow of our conversation, and all the peaceful thoughts I had as we lay together in bed. I remembered Milo's sad-looking face right before I left his apartment building. I remember wanting to apologize, to hear the album he worked so hard on. But what was he up to these days? I didn't even check up on Milo since I tagged him in a post about the article on Facebook. That's what led me to search for his name.

At first, I thought I'd find Milo the same as I left him. Honestly, I believed he might've realized being a "starving artist" was not so glamorous and found a real job. It was the best hope I could've asked for—I wanted Milo to be okay, especially with the pandemic. But his Facebook profile had disappeared. No matter how long I searched, it was impossible to see him anywhere.

Trying to remain calm, my focus centered on looking up class lists from our high school, Montreal clubs, Montreal DJs, and so much more in between. Nothing. And it was around then I became concerned. Besides, what if Milo got COVID-19 and passed away? What if he was now gone from the face of the earth and I didn't get a chance to say goodbye? I almost wanted to call his parents to see if he moved back home. But yet, it was those dark perceptions that made me remember the name of Milo's debut album—*Joie de Vivre*. I even remembered a few song titles like "Fall Vibes", "Rhythmic Chills", "Joie de L'Été", "Peace on the Floor", and "Montréal, ma grande, grande amor". Despite everything, the names of Milo's songs had been well thought out.

Before I went on YouTube to further my investigation, I didn't know what I was hoping to discover. Looking back, I expected Milo to have a page with little activity, no engagement, and maybe a hundred views at best. I typed in "Milo Joie de Vivre" with no expectations. But the results that came back were far beyond what I imagined. I couldn't have predicted it if I tried.

Chapter 3

February 19, 2021

After researching Milo's life that week, I couldn't believe how successful my friend had become. Milo's Instagram, Facebook, and TikTok accounts were now under the name DJ Milo Joie and had millions of followers on each platform. There was travel content from all parts of the globe, Insta reels and videos that captured the madness of popular festivals, DJ sets in front of big crowds, pictures with the hottest celebrities and recording artists in the business, and a loyal fan base who showed their love for him by shares and concert videos that Milo often put on his Insta stories. It also turned out "Joie de Vivre" was the beginning of it all based on an interview Milo did on a podcast—a start he predicted at his old apartment. The craziest part was that Milo looked exactly the same. Other than nicer clothes, hair dyed every other week (which he admits proudly in a TikTok video as "Joie de Fame"), and a complexion that only hours in the sun and a proper skincare routine can bring. Milo was still the man I considered my first love.

Milo was now living his dream. He was a fantasy—a celebrity, a model-like figure that reflected the gods themselves. He was someone I pictured myself with behind closed doors. But I knew I had missed my chance. After all, if I stayed to listen to Milo's demo of "Joie de Vivre", maybe I would've become a part of his exciting lifestyle. Maybe I wouldn't be miserable in quarantine—or, at the least, it would have been spent down in the South of France, Rio de Janeiro, Belgium waiting for Tomorrowland to come back, Miami with hopes of

Ultra, Spain, Croatia, Thailand, Bali, or wherever else. All I could do was envy a success I once thought wasn't possible. I was just like most of Milo's followers—living through him online.

Listening to his songs on repeat, I realized there was an endless stream of heart, beauty, and grit behind the music—giving it a punch and a euphoric feeling. It wasn't the kind of sound you'd hear on a radio's top 40 hits. No, Milo reflected a special artist you'd discover naturally after clicking around online long enough. He was someone you'd only know if you were heavily invested in EDM. Dark lyrics were matched with uplifting rhythms to keep everything balanced.

The songs "Montréal, ma grande, grande amor", "Joie de l'Été", and "Fall Vibes" dove straight into his French-Canadian upbringing and the happiness he felt once he escaped his troubled home life for a world just beyond the Quebec town his family came from. The songs "Rhythmic Chills" and "Peace on the Floor" were reminiscent of his starving artist days as he strived to go forward. Everything Milo expressed to me was true. The album Milo once had so much faith in delivered with its artistry. The verses painted the canvases of his soul. The uplifting beats made you want to dance. Honestly, I listened to both his albums—the third was "on the way" according to an interview he gave with *DJ Mag*. I remember feeling that I needed to go for a walk before my head spun out of control. But as I left, I followed Milo on Instagram and liked his page on Facebook. I even went as far as creating a TikTok account to follow him.

Exploring my neighborhood for what felt like the millionth time, I remember seeing the familiar aura of isolation and loneliness around the block. Signs that read *"Ca va bien aller"* with a rainbow in the background were being promoted at the front of homes and apartments, yet nobody came to tell you it'll be "okay". Nobody wanted to say the words, regardless if they meant it or not. Every time I strolled by neighbors and people I knew, we'd quickly cross the street—avoiding contact and the possibility of being infected. I felt especially bad for the dogs. I was friends with two in my area, yet no longer was I allowed to pet them. A nod and an "I'm sorry" was all I got from their owners. The energy just wasn't there. Honestly, it was depressing to experience. And because of the pandemic, I wasn't sure if it would be the same ever again.

Despite it all, though, I enjoyed getting out of my studio apartment. I relished the feeling of being outside, not surrounded by darkness—only the sun as it reflected a glimmer of life to an otherwise dying world. The stars at night were prettier and more visible since there weren't as many people driving their cars and polluting the air with smoke from exhaust pipes. It was for those reasons and more that I always turned off my phone's data to immerse myself in the experience without any type of distraction. My notifications and text messages could wait, I thought. It was a great sense of freedom. But twenty minutes after this particular walk, I returned home to find an unexpected surprise waiting for me once my Wi-Fi connection was reactivated.

Not only did Milo follow me back on Instagram right away, but he tagged me in a post that highlighted my old feature article, liked half of my photos, and sent me a direct message. I also received ten new followers based on his post—they thought I was a "journalist" and wanted a feature themselves. Out of the ten, four of them even had a blue check mark and were artists one considered "rising stars". The attention felt overwhelming. But it was the dm Milo sent me that left the greatest impact. Even now, I'm moved by the thoughtful construction of the words.

"Hey, brother! Long time no see, eh? I've been doing pretty good, as you can probably tell! I'm actually super-pumped that you found me because I could use some help from someone I love and respect. I attribute part of my success to you based on the belief you once showed me with the article and wanting to reach out. I hope you're doing great, btw! I know it's been hard on all of us dealing with covid bullshit. But anyway, hit me back when you can. We'll catch up."

At first, Milo's immediate response confused me. It almost seemed like he waited for me to find him this whole time. Famous people like Milo hired teams of expert digital marketers, copywriters, videographers, and content creators to deal with that noise. But knowing Milo the way I did, I couldn't deny that it was he who wrote the message. I remember feeling hesitant writing back to Milo that night. It felt like I reawakened the innocence once felt inside of me whenever I was around Milo in my youth. Suddenly, I was a university student again trying so hard to be "normal". But my taste for nostalgia was heightened during the pandemic—that's something I learned. And even though it is usually best to move forward in life, I found it impossible. Memories shared with Milo had a place in my heart. It made me see I couldn't let go.

Quarantine had a way of making me feel alone with my thoughts, since visits with others were pretty much nonexistent. I was vulnerable, a victim to the loves I didn't know were still present in my heart. It scared me to reignite a spark with Milo. What good and bad ideas would come forth once again if I were to explore that part of myself? But despite all that, it didn't take me very long to recognize Milo was determined to recapture something precious about us, something he never forgot about even for a second. He was excited and happy when I answered.

"Hey, my dude! Yeah, it has been a while!" I wrote to Milo. "It's good to talk to you again, bro. And I'm so glad that you're doing so well in life. I mean… damn, this is wild. You made it happen! Everything you told me came true. You're a celebrity and I had no idea. LMAO."

"Thank you so much, brother! It really means a lot. And once I saw you follow me back, I knew I couldn't let this moment slip away. I learned in life that it can be easy to lose contact with people. And now with covid, we're suddenly craving other humans more than ever. It's so funny to me hahahahahaha. I'm telling you… people don't know what they have until it's gone."

"How have you been holding up btw?" I wrote, knowing how accurate and universal his thoughts were. "Since clubs and bars aren't open like they used to be, it's gotta be hard for you."

"Nah, my dude! Everything is actually better than ever, believe it or not. I've used all my time off from live performances to FINALLY work on my third album. Maybe Canada and the US are doing bad, but other parts of the world are getting through this pandemic shit differently."

"Guess a well-traveled guy like yourself would know hahahaha! But can you explain that more? Idk what you mean, like are you saying there's a way for you to perform again or what?"

"Yeah, brother, it's manageable af in other parts of the world now. I've gone to Mexico recently, Costa Rica, and also Miami. I feel like other countries will wake up by August, but holy shit! Aren't you Mexican on your dad's side? If I remember correctly? You need to come with me and my team next time we go. It's fucking wild now since there aren't many covid rules, and people can actually have a sense of life! Everyone is escaping the pandemic bullshit in Playa Del Carmen, Tulum, Cancun, and pretty much everywhere else. I'm planning a big show in Playa to promote my new music, brother. Or maybe some place more intimate with fewer tourists, idk yet. People need human connection again, that's just it! And I'm going to make that happen!!!"

Milo rambled on and on about Mexico like a drunk teenager. I didn't really get the hype at the time. After all, I was so used to lockdowns, curfews, and new outbreaks I never considered for a second that other parts of the globe had a different approach to the pandemic. I started to think of *mi familia* in Mexico, the cousins I haven't seen in years, the beaches and food I loved since childhood. Milo appeared to be the source of light I needed by bringing back those memories. I wanted to return to Mexico, to eat a taco and drink mezcal with my feet in the sand.

"I like the enthusiasm! But, honestly, based on the articles I read, I don't think people are going to magically forget about covid," I replied. "If it'll be possible to go see a show by August like you said, though, I will be there! Or at least I'll try to be if I can. That much I can promise."

It took Milo a while to answer. Several times he'd begin to write and delete his texts, shown by the jumping bubbles on the screen. I figured Milo had something important to say yet needed to word it right. It was obvious he was thrilled we reconnected—a hope and genuine love that leaped from my phone with everything that I read. About thirty minutes later, he wrote back.

"Brother, even if live shows won't be possible soon, I'll have one anyway at a penthouse rooftop or something cool like that. I feel like I'll be able to do it in Mexico either way because it's so fucking chill down there. Remind me, though, aren't you Mexican? Or Colombian? Argentinian? I remember you spoke Spanish with your dad, so yeah haha! It's driving me crazy."

"Yeah, I'm half Mexican! Remember how my parents used to shout 'VIVA MEXICO' every time I had the ball? Lmaooo they'd also say '*de la chingada*' and '*vamanos chicos*' a lot."

"Oh god, haha! Yeah, that's true, eh?! Even if someone else scored, they'd chant that."

"I also think I was the only Mexican on the team, so it was embarrassing."

"Nah, brother! Your parents love you. And as you know, not everyone has that. Let's just say my parents and I haven't talked in ages. Even with my success. It's not like I chose to be who I am. But I was smart and brave enough to see what God gave me! That's what counts the most if you want my opinion. Be authentically who you are, and the world will open the hell up."

"Honestly, I still remember the interview we did and what you went through before the fame. I'm glad to see you killing it like you are now! Really, it's incredible. You better keep it up, so one of these days I can see you perform live. I don't think I have yet, so it'll be awesome."

"It feels like a distant memory, but it also doesn't! And even though it sucked that you left me that day before I showed you my first demo, it didn't stop me from keeping the good times alive. You just said it, right?! We played soccer, we had a meaningful friendship, and experienced a lot together. Look, I don't mean to come off strong because I know what we had is done... but I loved when we banged. Now *that* was perfect! Anyway, though, I realize you have a girlfriend. I'm cool with being friends—actually, I prefer it. The less drama, the better, haha!"

Reflecting on things now, it seemed Milo wasn't over our flame—a spark that I believed died. I was still his teenage and forever crush. But the more we spoke, the more I anticipated his DMs, and that just reminded me more of the world that took shape when Milo and I were together. It was intimate and real. Better than any relationship I ever had. And with that level of comfort in mind, I became more vulnerable. Suddenly, I wanted to be with Milo—to be in his arms, to embrace him, to give him my heart. I wanted to see him in my room, not on my phone.

"Oh, I haven't had a girlfriend in a while," I replied. "I dated one when I was at uni as you know, but we ultimately decided it wasn't going to work anymore. Maybe the sex wasn't as good as I thought, or we didn't have that much in common. It happens all the time, I guess... it's life."

"Yeah, or maybe... I was always in the back of your mind."

I smiled at that moment, knowing he wasn't entirely wrong.

"Maybe you're on to something! It's hard to describe why I like who I like most times."

"Trust me, brother, I see people hook up all the time when I play at clubs and bars and festivals. You should see it for yourself, dude. It's possible to see how beautiful strangers come together from start to finish. You analyze the body language and eventually sense if two people are going to make out or whatever. It's funny because I've seen rejections happen ten minutes before they happened and vice versa. And you know what's crazy, man? The ability to learn how to read dance floors follows you. So... I'm able to feel that something between us still lingers."

"Even if you're right, quarantine and the fact you're a celebrity will make it impossible for us to recreate. You can have anyone you want. So, why me? I'm an unemployed uni graduate with nothing going on. And I'm pretty sure I'm beginning to gain a little weight, so yeah, lmao."

Once more, Milo took a while to respond—writing and deleting his words, trying to craft the perfect text. I felt humbled someone out there cared so much about what I thought. He wanted to make me smile. He wanted me to feel better about myself. I realized then that there was a chance Milo was "the one". All it took was a pandemic to see what was most important.

"No need to be embarrassed, brother!" Milo wrote. "I'm into you, not what you do. That bullshit doesn't express who you are deep inside, anyway. People change all the fucking time, so being tied to one idea or one job would just be soul-crushing. So, like… the key is to just do what you love presently. Not what you used to love or what you hope to love, but what makes your heart leap from your chest *now*. Don't define yourself by a "job" or a "career", brother. It's a short life we've got, so don't waste it on being tied down. Be free and be your most authentic you! And hey, it's probably good that you're not in an office because we can talk more, hahaha."

"I appreciate your kindness and lack of judgment, man! I wouldn't expect anything less from you, but I need an income, and fast. It's true I have to do what I love, but it's really hard to break into journalism. Unless you know someone who is in the business, it is nearly impossible."

"But you're so talented! I don't understand it, brother. I just fucking don't, honestly."

"Talent isn't experience. And I'm not the only person who's got it, so it's more about competition. I'm telling you, every time I apply for something, I'm against fifty other people."

"Speaking of which, that reminds me…I might have a solution for your problem. And, it's the reason I was quick to reconnect with you again. Well, other than the fact you're a hottie."

Between you and I, that's when Milo's sweet talk made me blush.

"What's up?" I wrote back with anticipation and shaky hands.

"I could really use some publicity going into the big shows I'm doing in Playa Del Carmen. It's going to be madness since I'll be promoting new songs and mixes, like I said before already. And it will include posts with sneak peeks, captions, and things like that—shit that'll get fans excited. I was hoping you'd be interested in helping me since you're from my hometown. It would be so dope to get the word out from a local voice. People eat that up! That's the reason I shared our article. I wanted to create momentum for you and for others to see it for themselves."

"Damn, bro, you're awesome... what an incredible opportunity! It would be an honor."

"Yeah, anytime! I can't think of anyone that's more deserving. Not many people knew me before the fame. I cherish that since it will be refreshing to be treated as a normal guy again."

"I can't wait to get started, man!" I was super excited. "It's going to be amazing."

"I'm glad to hear that enthusiasm, brother! Anyway, I have to record some music now. My producer and sound engineer just arrived and we're going to film the process, so it's going to be *fuego*! I'll hit up my team about putting you on the payroll, so keep checking on your inbox."

Right then, my heart raced with anticipation. I couldn't help but cherish the moment as it came, welcoming the rush of nostalgia and past dreams as they manifested into a promising future. I was evolving and heading toward my next chapter with every minute of conversation. It seemed my future was with Milo. But although I was grateful, a dread filled me I couldn't shake. It felt as though my heart was both excited and terrified. However, I wasn't in a position to refuse Milo's kindness. I needed a job, and he provided it. During COVID-19, it was a godsend.

Chapter 4

August 5, 2021

Working on Milo's team kept me busy for the last six months, and I loved every minute. I was a contracted freelance "Brand Copywriter" who wrote social media posts, replied to DMs and comments, helped to create email newsletter campaigns, and even wrote blog articles that went into detail about Milo's latest news, which included a breakdown of his new songs, travel destinations, tour date info, and so much more. I became part of Milo's company "Joie Media".

Surprisingly, it was an organization with fifty people that were all dedicated to keeping Milo's online presence fresh, relevant, and exciting for his audience. And from the moment they announced my name in a LinkedIn post as Joie Media's newest hire, I quickly made professional connections I never would've gotten by myself. Everyone who worked for Milo reached out to congratulate me on joining their "family", welcomed me on the team, and encouraged me to ask questions I might've had about the company. It was overwhelming at first, yet I got used to the hustle. I gained work experience, felt more corporate than ever, and collected a solid paycheck.

For the first time in my post-university life, I didn't have to stress about my finances. It was an indescribable feeling of relief I can't explain. But I also learned what it meant to work for a celebrity like Milo behind the blue check mark. I did things from writing punchy one-line captions to selecting a photo out of five to post online. I had input on longer blog articles whenever Milo felt deep and spiritual (which happened at least once a week). He loved to give his fans a detailed look into his love for music, DJing, and beach life. More importantly, Milo was great at illustrating his eagerness to perform for his audience. Yes, as I learned quickly, Milo was a master at creating vibrant online communities. Every post included a storm of comments.

What I loved most about working alongside Milo was getting to communicate with him like we did in the past. Funny enough, it felt like we were partners in a high school project by the way we talked to each other. We'd be serious for about an hour and then reminisce about soccer, teachers we had, funny memories, and Montreal hotspots we both enjoyed in our youth. It was all going so smoothly, and I couldn't have asked for a better start to my "writing career". I grew my online network by 100 people while being associated with some of the biggest names in the entertainment industry—millionaires that I would never have had the chance to meet otherwise.

Despite all that, though, I didn't enjoy working from 10:00 a.m. to 6:00 p.m., five days a week. There was no time for anything else other than my "home office". But everyone on Milo's team embraced the "lifestyle" of working for a celebrity, often working extra unpaid hours when it wasn't a requirement. In fact, there were moments I felt judged for wanting to log off at 6:00 p.m. to eat dinner. Looking back, there was something wrong with the culture that Milo's team set. But I told myself "You're new and need to prove your worth". So, I'd work late hours too. After all, I was lucky to even have a job in the economy COVID-19 destroyed. Unemployment was common— at least in Canadian news—and I didn't want to rely on government subsidies forever. Maybe Milo knew that. But it was hard to see what's clear now.

That summer, our main project was to highlight Milo's next Mexico tour dates for the end of this year. Even though we needed to be careful with how we approached it, Milo wanted to remain optimistic, strategic, and creative with the planned content he wanted to post. He paid digital marketing experts a shitload of money to help us figure it out. The last thing Milo wanted was any backlash from his audience, a major news publication, or something along those lines.

For the next couple of months, we planned to have little snippets of Milo's new music on his social media pages, along with footage of shows he did over the years. According to Joie Media's software, that kind of content performed well no matter what time you posted it online. The Instagram reels were also going to be filled with endless travel content and inspirational quotes Milo said in feature interviews, podcasts, and things of that nature. But the song we needed to push most was his upcoming single that August—a single called "Bumble Dreams".

I was blown away when I heard it. In fact, Milo tapped me to write a blog article regarding his thoughts on the song's creation. Strangely enough, there was something about it that resonated deep within me. It was about how unexpected it could be to meet someone on a dating app, how energy is energy no matter where it comes from, and the beauty of a real connection. It seemed as though Milo wrote the song with a certain person in mind. But the most interesting thing was that it was a last-minute edition. Milo came up with the single days earlier and put it on the new album. During our company-wide meeting, everyone was raving about it.

* * * *

"All the great ones have breakthroughs like this," Lisa Flemings said, the head digital marketing expert on Milo's team. She liked my job announcement on Joie Media's LinkedIn page, but that was the extent of our relationship. I was at the bottom of the corporate ladder, and she was a heavyweight. We had nothing in common. She probably didn't even know my name.

"John Lennon used to come up with songs in dreams, and Lynyrd Skynyrd wrote "Sweet Home Alabama" before their first album even came out. It's just a testimony to the music gods and how sometimes they decide to bless a worthy, talented artist like our Milo. What do you guys think about that? Please, I'd love to know your thoughts. Feedback is always appreciated."

Everyone part of the company was in that meeting, yet I couldn't remember all their faces. Some people mentioned we could leverage Milo's "greatness" by getting him to talk about John Lennon being one of his favorite artists. One person noted how, when Kanye West collaborated with Paul McCartney, young kids on Twitter had no idea who The Beatles' pop star was and mistakenly thought Kanye discovered him. But it resulted in a social media interest in The Beatles, so the idea was placed under consideration. More people suggested we find venues around Mexico that were safe enough and would let Milo perform a live show. Not everyone on Milo's team was comfortable with that goal. Several worried COVID-19 was something not to be downplayed. And although Mexico was *"chill af"* as Milo defined it, a big percentage of our audience came from Canada, the United States, the UK, and other parts of the world that still had issues related to the pandemic. It was important for us not to offend them in any shape or form.

Since we were approaching September, Milo dreamed of creating an escape for his fans. For many, traveling to see him perform was half the fun. It was a vacation energy Milo's audience thrived on. He was determined to revive their partying spirits. That became his main focus.

But even then, would people come out to see Milo perform in Mexico after the shitshow of 2021? Did Milo's following have the money to travel? At the end of the day, Milo was the boss and had a *"no pasa nada"* attitude he picked up from his first Mexico tour last February and March of this year. It got Milo to encourage us all to be more positive and "solution-oriented".

Eventually, the meeting shifted to this question: how could we promote Milo's Mexican shows without discouraging fans in pandemic-affected countries? Since it was complicated to answer, nobody on the team had good ideas to share. But right before we lost hope, a beautiful face appeared on the screen. One of the social media managers from Mexico spoke for the first time. And she had an energy that radiated through my laptop. It captured my attention with ease.

"Maybe we can do a video before Milo's performances *y despues podemos* show this to the people who have interests," Diana Romero said, a little unconfident with her English yet brave enough not to let it get the best of her. She was one of the few people at Joie Media who didn't have a LinkedIn presence. Her main platform was Instagram since photography was a specialty as well as a genuine passion. But nobody could deny her talent. "We could gather small groups and do a *fiesta* Mexican style. Bring the experience to people if they cannot show there with us."

"Oh, interesting! So, it would be a pre-recorded video that would demonstrate a concert-like setting?" Lisa asked, nodding her head. "Well, okay! I like the idea of that because we would have full control over the party's reaction. It would be a music video shoot or something."

"Exactamente que si!" Diana said, very upbeat. "So, if people see the video, they will engage. We can show the vibes and music all over the place. I also see DJs online do live stream alone in front of the nice views, so maybe we can do this also for Milo. It looks good online, and it can be only with Milo, *tu entiendes*? He can do this little show and it will feel like a concert."

"Okay, sounds awesome," Lisa said. "I like your forward thinking. Anyway! That'll be it for everyone today. I'll report back to Milo sometime later tonight and then confirm our next steps."

There was something about Diana's character that I gravitated to before I could even understand its meaning. It was how she expressed her opinion. There was a fire in her soul. I was drawn to her smile and the degree to which her brown eyes lit up once everyone supported her ideas—for staying true to herself and being courageous enough to speak. But most of all, I liked her little Spanglish moments. It reminded me of the way I talked *con mis padres y familia* in Mexico. And I was comfortable with Diana, even though we haven't met or had a conversation. I realized then that perhaps I should look up Diana Romero on Instagram. After all, I had a good reason. What I found was nothing short of remarkable—enhancing my curiosity even further.

Diana had over 5,000 Instagram followers and was a "photographer, videographer, nature lover, and explorer of all things food and art related", according to her bio. There were more photos of mountain tops, beaches, street food stalls, museums, art galleries, and everyday people in Mexico and neighboring Latin American countries than there were of her. But the ones that did feature Diana were some of the most beautiful. I was becoming obsessed without recognizing it. And once I scrolled through numerous photos, I sent her a follow request and a nice message.

In the back of my head, I knew a thousand people likely texted Diana every single day—perhaps guys who hoped to take her out on a date. But I had an incentive. I was connected to Diana through Milo. So, I wrote this very briefly: "*Hola, Diana! Me llamo Max Velasco. Soy Canadiense y trabajo con Milo también.* I loved your ideas in the Zoom meeting today and I'm looking to meet other people on the Joie Media team. *Espero que podemos ser amigos. Mi familia es Mexicana, pero naci en Montreal. Hablo bien en Spanglish!* Anyway, get back to me whenever you can. Maybe I'll see you soon if your idea *por una fiesta* Mexican style happens."

Afterward, I turned off my laptop and set my phone on "Do Not Disturb" for the rest of the night. I didn't want to feel the pain of Diana leaving me on "read". But strangely, I also didn't have as strong a desire to get an immediate reply from Milo anymore. Ever since I began work, I always felt excited to see what Milo had on his mind throughout the weeks. But two minutes of Diana made me feel indifferent to what Milo had to say—no matter how charming or funny it might have been. I was confused by the storm of emotions I already felt for Diana yet assumed that my innocent crush would fade after a day or two. God, I was never more wrong in my life.

Chapter 5

September 18, 2021

During the course of a month, I talked to Diana more and more. It turned out we both had the same taste in food. She loved avocados, tacos, and *pescado*. But mostly, we liked the idea of meeting each other in Mexico. It was an intense feeling I don't know how to describe. Even though we haven't physically been in touch, I felt a strong connection to Diana as if we've been friends for a long time. I loved the way she used emojis—from smiley faces, winks that conveyed playfulness, fire signs, and even her choice of hand gestures that included the "Okay" and "Call me" signs. There was something fun about her character. It was childish to a degree, yet it was also intensely engaging. She was able to illustrate good energy in her texts. I was never bored with the conversations that I had with her. I missed her each time I waited for a response.

But I also wasn't sure how long things would last. The month of August was stressful for Milo, and it was something that impacted our team. We all felt the realities of COVID-19, politicians, and healthcare professionals' rule against Milo's creative process when it came down to our planned content, vision for blogs, and the messaging he wanted to express to his audience.

The darkness that began in March 2020 was still present going into the fall of 2021. Festival season in Montreal was nowhere to be found. Major shows like Tomorrowland and Ultra were canceled and many other parts of the globe didn't see their nightlife come back into the picture. It was depressing, yet that was the main point our team brought up to Milo—posting about "good vibes only" wasn't appropriate considering the struggles our fan base was going through.

From what I heard, the final cut of Milo's album didn't live up to his standards either. And this led him to announce the news to his fans in an Instagram reel video. Milo even got me to write a press release on his social media pages about the new album's delay for media outlets to pick up if they were interested. Surprisingly, a handful of DJ magazines ran with it— leading to a lot of comments of reassurance that supported Milo's decision. It was admirable of him to care that much about people online he'd never meet. I didn't know anyone who carried the kind of hope Milo did. But yet, one of the biggest reasons behind Milo's setbacks was his thoughts regarding his beloved Canadian fanbase. There were many people from Quebec and other parts of Canada that happily frolicked to see Milo no matter where he performed. It was to the point where Milo refused to do anything without his "Fellow Canadians" and *"Pouchons"*. Everything was at a standstill. Worst of all, Milo didn't communicate with us much in September. Nobody knew what was going to happen. But Diana's perspective changed how I looked at the situation.

"The true artist is never satisfied, they care too much," Diana texted me that night. "It is complicated because nobody truly understands. I like to make art *con mi* laptop, *mi energía, y mi cámara*, so I know what it is like to fight to create beautiful things. But if you do not experience, you are not a true artist and have no art to share *con gente*. Nobody must understand you, no? And if I were *famosa como* Milo, then it matter more to be good. It is all that you have to give."

"Yeah, I didn't look at it like that. Idk, *tal vez* Milo *tiene muchas cosas en su mente*."

"Claro que sí, wey!" Diana replied. "Imagine having millions *de gente* enjoy you always. Trust me, *Milo* will create the art he loves eventually. But *con la pandemia, todo es complicado*."

* * * *

Looking back, I was tired of people saying that. I knew just as well as the next person that the pandemic made everything "complicated", yet it was also frustrating to wait as life passed me by without many improvements. The vaccine helped, yet there were still lockdowns in place by September in Montreal. What was going on in Canada, I thought? It seemed as though *joie de vivre* was gone. And knowing winter was coming, my seasonal depression made things worse.

Despite that, however, I chose not to lay my internal struggles on Diana. Currently, she was in Tulum and far away from the madness of pandemic troubles. I wanted to maintain a positive attitude that matched hers. Ranting to her about Montreal would have ruined our banter.

"Anyway, you know what I realize now?" Diana texted, out of nowhere. "I went to school *con tus primos*! *Pregunté ellos en la semana última, y ellos saben quien eres*. I know Hugo, Sara, and Manuel. But I hang out with Sara most because we are the same age. We used to listen to *la musica* and talk about the boys. It has been a long time since I see them, but I hope that changes. I also know Manuel. He dated *amigas yo tengo jaja*. Small worlds as they say in English, *no*?"

"Wait, are you sure?" I texted back, unable to believe the coincidence.

"Yes, *Maxito*! The reason I also know is because *yo vi un foto en* Instagram *con tu y* Bellita. I see her in *las fotos con* Hugo, Sara, y Manuel *tambien* in the holidays, so I put it all together."

All of a sudden, a powerful sense of joy entered my heart. It felt like I was having a stroke. The nostalgia I received from the idea of Bellita brought me to tears while I stared at my phone. I knew what photo Diana was referring to since it depicted my last visit to Mexico. It was back in 2012, once my second year of high school had finished. My parents thought it'd be nice for me to spend the summer in Mexico City with my cousins. I lived in my uncle Jose's house—*Casa Velasco,* as we liked to call it. I loved spending time there and eating my aunt Clarisa's food.

Honestly, 2012 was a confusing time in my life. I struggled to understand who I was from a sexuality point of view. Some days, I thought I was gay because I looked up male celebrities on my laptop when everyone else in the house would be asleep. Other times, I'd think about the pretty girls at my school just like every other straight male. I couldn't decide who I preferred most, and it impacted my mental health. I felt insecure and embarrassed since it was hard to find someone to talk to about my vulnerabilities. But it was that summer I first met Isabelle Velasco.

Smiling as I write this down, it was the start of a beautiful relationship I'd forever cherish. People in our *familia* used to call her "Bellita" for short. She was the young daughter of a relative on the Velasco family tree yet wasn't close with Jose and Clarisa's side until mid-2012. I still recall the heaviness in the air when Bellita was taken in at Casa Velasco. Despite that Bellita was only eleven, she was going through a dark time most people would never understand.

Bellita had many challenges in her life since she was born with down syndrome. From learning disabilities to major health problems, she had a lot of things to overcome. But in early 2012, she lost her parents in a car accident in Monterrey. At the time, Jose took her in until her grandmother returned to Mexico City from Oaxaca. I remember how everyone felt tense and delicate around her. Bellita was too young to realize what was going on. But she was an extravert, which meant she liked to make friends, play, and interact. Everyone else in Casa Velasco tried to give her space because they didn't know how to explain to a young child the realities of her new world. But since I only knew ten words of Spanish back in high school, I was the perfect candidate to play games with her whenever it got too uncomfortable for others in the house. We had battleship duels, played *Monopoly*, and even traded Pokémon cards. But for some reason, our favorite game was *Connect Four*. And each time Bella won, she'd do a little dance.

After a while, our bond grew so much that I'd go with her to the local *mercado* alongside Jose and Clarisa. We'd get ice cream twice a week. We walked around the mall. Looking back, I even remember learning Spanish with each interaction I had with Bellita, as she'd ask me questions or point out things *en al mercado* she enjoyed. I met her favorite vendors and artisans— all of which loved to engage in conversations about the day, food, and everything in between with her. Bellita enjoyed giving out compliments, and she'd usually get free samples because of her grace. The vendors used to call her *"La Reina"*, which Bellita embraced with pride. Eventually, I discovered she was trying to learn English so we could talk more. She even kept a notebook in her room, always practicing her verbs and common phrases. I was touched by the effort she made. It rubbed off on me as the summer progressed. And during the last week of my stay in Mexico City, I was able to speak passable Spanish, and she was able to speak English.

Don't get me wrong, I loved my other cousins. In fact, I sometimes talked to them on Facebook or commented on their Instagram stories. But the relationship with Bellita was special. It even showed in our enthusiasm to play *Connect Four* against each other. Slowly, Bellita would open herself up to me and I would tell her about life in Montreal. It was cute and quite innocent.

But before too long, my last day in Mexico City arrived— leading Bellita to tears. It took forever to calm her down, after endless promises that I'd return to Mexico for the holidays. I recall thinking everything would be okay. Until 3:00 a.m. came on the night of my departure.

"Maxito, Maxito," Bella whispered, as she tapped my head. *"Puedes despertar?"*

"Yes, *si,* I'm awake," I said, half-asleep. "Do you... *Necesitas algo importante?"*

"Vamos a jugar antes que te vayas!" Bella said, shaking the *Connect Four* box.

When I got out of bed, we headed down to the living room and played our usual "Best of 3 series". I won the first round, yet Bellita won the next two. It was competitive and engaging, as per usual. But it was around the start of our tenth game she told me something I'd never forget.

"Thank you for being friends," Bella said, as she was concentrating on her next move.

"Claro, prima," I said with a smile. "I'll always be your friend, no matter what."

"People, eh… sometimes are not… they believe I do not understand what happen *con mis padres.* But they are wrong. I miss *mi mama y papa* so much, but I know they like me happy. So… I am happy for them. I try to be very good for them in heaven. And you help me enjoy life."

"Again, n*o pasa nada,*" I said, not knowing how to respond. "But I'm still going to win."

"Never, never!" Bella said, laughing. "You can have dreams, but they are not realities."

At 4:10 a.m., we finished our last *Connect Four* series. Bellita won the majority of them, and she danced for what seemed like hours. Even though we had a good time, I was also exhausted and told her I'd see her at breakfast. Before I could go upstairs to pass out, however, she pulled me back. Bellita looked at me with an expression that demanded my full presence.

"Do you like to be near girls, or is it the boys?" Bella asked me with genuine interest.

"Why *tienes esta pregunta*?" I replied after a long pause. Suddenly, my hands were shaking.

"No se, but I see you talk nicely to *el hombre* that gives ice cream and it remind me of Hugo and Manuel *con sus novias* they had before. Do you have *secretos* or do people only behave like this inside of Canada? I am very curious, *primo.* I hope that you can tell me anything you want."

Unable to breathe, I didn't understand the magnitude of this exchange while it happened. It was funny how Bellita saw through me like that. But since the rest of *la familia* avoided talking about her grief, I could also see through Bellita too. Somehow, we were linked in our troubles that were mostly kept deep inside. But neither of us was able to hide that particular night, and Bellita made sure of it. She wanted to know me better and felt that our relationship was strong enough to be real. And before I could dance around things, she continued with encouragement.

"Please, tell me as friends who you are," Bellita said. "I love you and want to know."

For a minute, I hesitated. I looked to see if anyone else in the house had woken up and come downstairs. But then Bellita reached for my hand—suddenly making me burst into endless tears.

"I do, *me gusta las mujeres*," I said, feeling a weight about to be lifted off my shoulders. "But I…I think I also like boys, as well. It's hard to talk about, so just don't tell anyone *en la familia*. Maybe it's a phase. I don't really know yet. But please, Bellita…this stays between us."

"Don't be *triste*!" Bellita said. "I accept and understand. I keep your secret forever."

Each of those memories came rushing back when I clicked on my #tbt Mexico photo I shared nine years earlier. I couldn't even recall the last time I spoke to Bellita. And suddenly, I thought of who she might've been playing Connect Four with during quarantine. Concern also grew about her health for some reason. Besides, it was just her and her grandmother in a small apartment forty-five minutes away from Casa Velasco. It seemed that I'd never reach Bellita ever again with how the world was shaping in 2021. But the universe can be interesting. Sometimes, it gives you what you need if you hope for something long enough. And reflecting on Bellita, Mexico City, and my sexual identity, I received an unexpected phone call from Milo.

"Pack your fucking bags, brother. You're going to Mexico!" Milo said, explicitly drunk. "I'm tired of being surrounded by depression and bad vibes. I can't even see people at my sweet Toronto condo anymore! I need more company, dude. So, I'm going to fly you out to Playa Del Carmen with our other North American-based team members. I decided to go with Diana's idea from before, so we're going to shoot a video to go with my planned tour dates. And I want you there for the shoot. It's going to be wild like tequila on the dance floor. So, I hope you're ready."

"Are you sure it's possible, though?" I replied, thrown off by Milo's proposition. Better yet, it seemed too good to be true. "I mean… I'm excited. But the world is kind of dark right now."

"Would I lie?" Milo said. "It's happening, brother. It's time to bring back the light."

Right then, I didn't know how to react. There was a lot to consider—my health, other people I may be in contact with, my life in Montreal, my little apartment, my past feelings for Milo, and the unpredictable nature of flying anywhere during a pandemic. Honestly, I wanted to jump on board without a second thought. And maybe, if this opportunity came my way before 2020, it would've been easier to pack up and leave. But I had every reason imaginable forcing me to decline Milo's course of action. The silence was unbearable as I juggled the options at hand. It's why I believe that COVID-19 was the universal headache of our time. Suddenly, most of the world's problems became more common. I didn't need to say anything to Milo for him to understand my dilemma on the phone. And it's when Milo spoke—helping me make a decision.

"Listen, the plan is completely safe. We're going to follow every precaution you can name, brother," Milo said in a serious tone. "And it won't be right away, so we're fine. It's going to take some time to find our location for the video, anyway. The plan is to have everyone in Mexico City by the end of September or early October, at the latest. Right after, we'll all quarantine for two weeks or however long it takes. I need to work out the details with the finance people on my team, but the good news is a handful of us are already in *Playa*. So, it's going to be fucking easy and painless. Once the quarantine is done, we'll get organized. But c'mon, let's get real. By next summer, this covid bullshit will be over. So, the goal is to hit up all the beaches in Mexico. I can already envision it being fire! I'm going to call the tour *Mexico Para Siempre*! I'm telling you, bro, it's going to be epic. So, what do you think? Are you in this with me or what?"

Initially, I thought Milo was delusional. I got the impression he was too invested in his dreams by the way he brushed off global issues that had impacted everyone to some degree. But selfishly, I would've rather spent the next round of lockdowns on a beach than in Montreal during the winter months. Mentally, that idea was in my head. Maybe I could've found time to see Bellita and *mi familia* in Casa de Velasco. Maybe I'd meet Diana for the first time. I hated myself for getting excited about great adventures when others struggled to keep their businesses afloat or their hopes for the future alive. There was a part of me that didn't even know why Milo would go through all this trouble. It appeared like an unnecessary risk. After all, I worked remotely and didn't need to do anything so extreme. But I was too distracted to see the red flags.

"Sounds pretty good, man," I replied after a brief pause. "But how is this going to work? Realistically, I'll probably be questioned by someone at the airport and I'm not too sure if my job is considered essential enough for travel standards. I mean… it's not like I'm a doctor or nurse."

"You're essential to me," Milo said blankly. "So, you'll make it to Mexico City, even if it means I'll have to fly you out myself. Trust me, brother, you're more valuable than you think."

Arrangements were made not long after our call finished. My parents were naturally apprehensive the next day when I told them what was happening. But it was Diana's excitement about the news on Instagram that really convinced me I was making the right choice for myself.

"OMMGGGG, *finalemente podemos tomar chelas!*" Diana texted me, quickly after I told her I was coming to Mexico. "No more Instagram! Can't wait to show you places. Mexico *es un sueño*. We can have real tacos, go see the artsss, and explore *mi ciudaddd*! You excited, wey?!?"

"*Si, no puedo esperar,*" I replied. "I can't wait to meet you too because it really needs to happen. We talk so much. And it'll be great since *yo no fui a México desde hace mucho tiempo*."

"We need to explore all the corners!" Diana said. "Mexico is a world to celebrate."

Genuinely, it was Diana's optimism that gave me the courage to make it to the airport. The risk of traveling during the pandemic era was taboo, but also exhilarating when I thought of all the memories I could make if I took the leap forward. It was a forgotten sense of adventure I was reminded of deep in my consciousness. Better yet, it was a feeling I wanted to chase forever.

Chapter 6

October 3, 2021

"Are you crazy?" my father yelled when I told him the news at dinner. "Do you have any idea how many *gente* are sick in Mexico? What are you thinking, Maxito? Don't be a *pendejo*."

Looking into his eyes, my father was dead serious. And it caught me off guard since he was the first person to congratulate me when I started to work for Milo's brand. Originally from *Guadalajara*, my father's parents migrated over to Toronto for the chance at a better life when he was a little kid. He grew up with strong values centered on hard work, family, and tradition that he carried over to our household. Honestly, I thought I was going to make my father proud when I explained my Mexico plans—honoring Milo, the company, and everyone else who relied on me to give it my best in the remote office. But at the dinner table, it seemed like my father didn't value my happiness. More so, it felt like he didn't see my growth as a young professional.

"I'm going for work, though, so it's not like I'm traveling just to travel," I replied. "And Milo is taking care of everything, so there's no need to worry. I'll be more than okay! *No pas—*"

"Not everything is about work!" my father snapped, cutting me off. "What about family? Jobs didn't save us from the pandemic. But we're blood. And that's what is most important."

Right there, I lost my appetite. It sucked how my father questioned my integrity like that.

"I never said family wasn't important! But everyone needs money to live, right? I'm doing what I got to do. Yeah, fine… maybe it's true I work a lot. But I also know I'll save a lot too."

"Work isn't your whole life, *Maxito*," he said. "It's not your one and only purpose."

"I'm still going to Mexico," I said. "I'd rather work there than be miserable in Montreal."

"Have you even read any of the news reports I sent you online?" my mother asked with a blank expression. I felt the deep concern in her voice. "No, probably not! If you did, maybe you'd make a smarter choice. Your father's right. What are you thinking? What if you get sick?"

"Yeah, I mean, do you have any idea what's happening?" Gabriella Velasco, my little sister, said. "I was going to go backpacking across Europe this summer, so how do you think I feel?"

"I get it, but I need to get out of Canada. I'm tired of quarantine and not being able to go outside unless it's for a walk, groceries, or something like that. I want a sense of normalcy again, you know? I can't stand this bullshit anymore. And thankfully, Milo feels the same way as I do."

"Well, guess what—everyone is tired of quarantine," my father said. "You don't think I miss going to the office or seeing my friends *por un café*? You don't think I miss going out to restaurants or *fútbol* games? I know I can't stop you from doing this. But don't be selfish! Don't even brag about it on your phone like kids do your age *de la chingada*! People will get very jealous and report you to the government. If we're mad and love you, imagine those who don't."

"It's true. You don't listen!" Gabriella said. "But fine, asshole, do whatever you want."

Shortly after, I left my parents' house feeling defeated. They had a point: everyone in Montreal felt just as miserable. But yet, I was the one who seemed lucky enough to get away from the pain that struck most Canadians in some form. Suddenly, I felt nauseous—so much so that I wanted to cancel my adventure to Mexico. But while I sat in my car, I saw my mother run out of the house with what looked like a small notebook in her hand. I remembered thinking it was strange. After all, my mother was a strong-willed person who rarely showed any kind of emotion. She looked everywhere, possibly thinking I had already left. I almost wanted to call her on my phone until we finally locked eyes. I rolled down my car window as she approached.

"We're still mad at you for being arrogant, irresponsible, and entitled, thinking it's fine to leave your family behind during a global pandemic," she said, as though what she held weighed over fifty pounds by the way her shoulders hunched forward. "But here... this is for Bellita."

"Sounds good." I felt awkward. "Is this a diary or something?"

"No, it's her language book from when she was in high school. Remember the Christmas your father and I visited the family when you were sixteen? The first thing Bellita wanted to do was practice her English so she could write you a postcard. Anyway, we kept her drafts in a notebook. It's something her parents taught her to do since she was five, and I wanted to honor that method. She learns through writing and memorization. Anyway, she became pretty good by the end. But she was embarrassed with her spelling and grammar, so please don't read a word. There's also a photo of all of us for her to keep... and I don't want it slipping out by accident."

For a minute, I thought my mother was trying to shame me even more for venturing off to Mexico City on short notice. But when I nodded, and she went back inside with a sense of relief, I knew that it meant the world to her I was going to reach Bellita with such a wholesome present.

When I got to my little apartment, I started to reflect on my mother and Bellita's relationship more. It seemed like a lifetime ago when my parents visited Mexico together. But then again, I also remembered the times my mother spoke glowingly about helping Bellita with homework. It occurred to me she had a relationship with her that was just as beautiful and wholesome as mine.

Proudly from a small town in Alberta, my mother's name is Melissa Gibson. After she graduated from high school, she moved to Montreal for university and met my father there— Carlos Velasco, an International Relations student with a passion for everything Latin America.

Back in the day, my mom was an Education Major with dreams of someday empowering young women. On the other hand, my dad was more focused on making a life for himself— no matter what kind of career he fell into. Both of them were from different worlds, yet my mom fell in love with my dad for his heart and enthusiasm toward the people he cared about most. Similar to my father, she was an outsider in Montreal. Better yet, she often felt excluded in certain parts of my dad's life, especially when she visited everyone at Casa Velasco for the first time in the summer after their junior year. From what I knew, it's how she met Bellita's parents.

They were educators in the Mexican public school system —the kind of people my mother dreamed of becoming in the future. When they generously offered her mentorship during her stay in Mexico City, it blossomed into a meaningful, professional relationship. They stayed in contact for years, always exchanging notes and ideas about teaching methods. By her senior year, my mom was able to communicate well in Spanish. She was even in the hospital when Bellita was born. If anyone knew how much Bellita's parents adored her, it was my mother.

Lovingly, they'd often refer to Bellita as a "little genius" since prominent figures like Albert Einstein, Nicola Tesla, and even Shakespeare were once misunderstood people who achieved great things. Bellita's parents believed in her potential more than anything in the world. So, when they died in that car accident, my mother felt she had a responsibility to help Bellita see that potential. For her master's, it inspired her to specialize in teaching children with special needs.

Before the pandemic, my parents tried to go back to Mexico City at least once a year to visit *la familia* and check up on

Bellita. She was essentially my mother's adopted Mexican daughter.

What troubled me most, however, was when my little sister, Gabriella, called me later that night to say Bellita hadn't answered her texts or messages for weeks. It turned out she became close with Bellita during the first wave of the pandemic, earmarking one of her "quarantine goals" to improve her Spanish. In all fairness, my sister also had a good relationship with our other three cousins. But there was something about Bellita's energy she couldn't ignore. Gabriella even confided she had FaceTimed numerous times with Bellita and her grandmother.

Suddenly, I recognized I had an obligation to my family—a mission to ensure Bellita was okay. I hoped to see her reaction to my mother's notebook, to practice my Spanish with her as she did her English. I wanted to play Connect Four. And I couldn't wait to take photos with her to ease my family's worries back in Montreal. Bellita's well-being correlated with my family's, and I couldn't let them down. But it also brought me to this conclusion: maybe I was meant to be this kind of hero, someone in a position to bring them a peace they couldn't get anywhere else.

PART 2:

FOREVER IN MEXICO

Chapter 7

October 16, 2021

When the Uber picked me up at 5:30 a.m., the excitement hit me that I was on my way to Mexico. It was strange considering how outlawed travel was at the time. All thoughts of my parents and Bellita were still fresh. But regardless, her notebook was packed in my bag with the kind of motivation you only get when you have the greatest intentions for the ones you love.

Strangely, my phone began to vibrate halfway to the airport. It caught me by surprise since most people were asleep at that hour. Even on the road, my Uber encountered no traffic. Naturally, I thought it was one of my coworkers telling me that our trip was canceled because of a border closure or something. That morning, I was supposed to meet people from the sales team, editorial, and a handful of videographers Milo hired full-time for the "music video/livestream" in Playa del Carmen or wherever we ended up in Mexico. But I decided it was too early to respond to anyone. Worst case, I'd see my Joie Media colleagues within an hour and deal with it then.

Honestly, I still remember how the airport resembled a ghost town. It seemed like happier times were behind the travel industry, and I saw the impact of the pandemic firsthand. Masks were mandatory, along with social distancing. But since there were almost no people around that morning, lineups at the front desks and security weren't crowded like it was pre-covid. I got through everything quickly, found a breakfast spot, and even bought a novel for the plane ride.

Walking until I found my plane tarmac, I munched on my egg wrap in anticipation of two things: meeting my coworkers for the first time outside of a video call, and texting Diana to let her know I'd be with her later that night. Looking back now, it was interesting to see all the faces I've encountered on my laptop screen, placing human energy on all the ones who reached out to me on LinkedIn to "message them anytime". They appeared welcoming and friendly online around the time I got hired at Joie Media. But when I saw them in person that morning, they resembled more of a popular high school clique, fazed by newcomers. Suddenly, I saw their "messages" for what they were—fake politeness embraced as a norm in the corporate world. They didn't want to be my "friend". No, they only reached out because it was expected of them.

They stared at me when I approached. Maybe it was because I looked exhausted. Or maybe I looked better or worse in person. I was about to break the ice with a polite greeting. Before that could happen, however, they beat me to the punch with something that caught me off guard.

"Hey, so when are you and Milo going to be official?" Jennifer said, one of the senior editors at Joie Media. She gave me feedback on my blog articles and posts, yet that was the extent of our relationship. And I got the feeling she was picking me apart at that moment as well.

"Yeah, we've been wondering that all morning!" Daniel said, a guy from the sales team. I remembered answering his simple 'Welcome to the company message' and then being ghosted.

"Sorry, what?' I replied, awkwardly. "Why... I mean, why even say that, though?"

For a while, the staring continued. It seemed like genuine curiosity to a degree. After all, they were smiling and telling me how "great a couple" Milo and I would be if we gave it a chance. I didn't get what was going on until a videographer named Christina opened her mouth.

"It was pretty obvious before," Christina said. "But today's post was way too out there."

Suddenly, I remembered the notifications from the Uber ride. And that's when I saw everything. "Through the ups and downs, @*Max.Velasco* was the pillar in my life who kept the rhythm in my heart going strong," Milo wrote in a morning post, which included a photo album of our high school days, one of us at a dinner table, and even one at my fifteenth birthday party I had long forgotten. "This beautiful man inspired me, wrote blog articles for me, and has done the best job helping keep my vision alive during this bullshit pandemic. Now, incredible surprises wait for you in *las playas* of Mexico. We're going to teleport you here with us! We can't wait to share!!! But for now, go to my bio and keep the love coming. Peace and happiness to you all!"

Milo made it sound like we had already become a couple. And the reason my phone was vibrating so much was that Milo's fans commented on the post—offering their "congrats" and "words of encouragement" with fire and heart emoticons. Looking back, it was the first red flag I couldn't ignore, a wake-up call that made me see I'd be making a huge mistake boarding that flight to Mexico. If it wasn't for Bellita's notebook, I would've taken an Uber home. But then, I scrolled through comments and found something that made me sweat: Diana liked Milo's post.

Since it wasn't even 7:00 a.m., I didn't think it was the best move to text Diana to clear things up. I wanted to see her in person. Besides, I was afraid she'd encourage Milo and me to be "together" like everyone else did on Instagram. Funny enough, I felt trapped in a one-sided love story. I should have listened to my parents and "made a smarter choice". But just when my head was about to explode with frustration, Milo sent me a nice message. It was right before the flight.

"Hey! I know my post was out there and shit, but I just wanted to express how happy I am that we'll be able to spend quality time together in paradise! Let me know when you arrive, brother. I promise it'll be the adventure of a lifetime. Nobody ever has a bad time in Mexico!"

Milo could have all the likes, reshares, and content in the digital landscape of our world. And with over 4.5 million Instagram followers, 3.2 million YouTube subscribers, and a million albums sold, it was clear from the beginning he was more of a celebrity than my best friend. He created DJ sets, dance parties, sparking memories and nostalgia in people through the music he created from scratch—even in depressing times. But once I sat in the plane about to take off to Mexico City, it became obvious the only "like" that Milo cared about was mine. It all made sense while re-listening to his music during the six-hour trip. The signs were everywhere. It even came from the short novel I bought at the airport bookstore: *"The Great Gatsby"*. It appeared like Milo was playing his version of Jay Gatsby in this scenario—a hopeful guy that had an idealistic view of the universe despite his many luxuries. On the other hand, I was "Daisy" since it was apparent he wanted us to be together. It was an idea of "happily ever after" only he saw.

But like Daisy, as I discovered less than an hour from Mexico City, I wasn't ready to give up my whole life just because Milo was foolishly convinced it was the right thing to do. It was a vision for us I didn't buy. I felt scared to death not knowing what would happen once the plane landed. Milo wanted to revisit something from our past. He wanted connection and romance—the type of emotions his music expressed. But it was unrealistic for me to give. And somehow, I thought the best way to show Milo we were never meant to be was to pursue Diana even harder.

Chapter 8

October 30, 2021

Even though I had to quarantine for two weeks at a hotel in downtown Mexico City, it felt incredible to be back in my second home. The view was magnificent: the beautiful artwork and color painted on the stone buildings, the architecture, and the people from my hotel window filled me with pride. My little sister, Gabriella, expressed her jealousy when she looked at my Instagram story that indicated I had arrived. Better yet, my parents and friends also reached out, wanting to know every detail of my adventure. It was in those moments I realized how lucky I was to have gotten out of Canada. Everyone was living precariously through me on their phones.

But reflecting on things now, it didn't bother me as it should have. There was good energy pouring into my soul, making me wish to be a part of Mexico's world. In my mind, I belonged here. And I couldn't wait to see *mi familia*, to visit Casa Velasco for the first time in a decade.

Little by little, my broken Spanish became more fluent. I found myself less stressed, letting go of the negativity that had crept up since the pandemic began. Now, able to explore the vibrant streets of downtown Mexico City once my quarantine period ended, I felt rejuvenated.

Funny enough, I was reminded of a few realities about Mexico City when I first landed. No matter where you are, the city's hot mess of reckless drivers, motorcyclists, drive n' texters, and lack of stop lights makes for a scary commute if you're not used to it. The food is also loved globally for a reason —whether it be tacos, quesadillas, enchiladas, or fresh mangos.

But mostly, one truth came to mind: don't believe everything the media tells you. Yes, the cartel isn't just something you find depicted on a show that you'll binge on a weekend. Maybe there are dark realities in the country to be aware of, like corrupt police and kidnappings. But when I visited Mexico in 2012, my father gave me this piece of advice: if you don't look for trouble, you won't ever find it. And as I presently rediscovered Mexico in 2021, I experienced moments of peace.

Mexico City, in all its inevitable charm and beauty, had over thirty million residents, good weather, and a unique sense of culture in the air. Staring out my hotel window, there were people from different backgrounds on the streets. It was a reminder of how open-minded and welcoming Mexico was. Nothing had changed since the last time I visited. Mexican Europeans, Muslims, Jewish people, Argentinians, Chileans, Venezuelans, American Expats, Canadians, and even Asian communities were everywhere once I walked around downtown Mexico City—*a centro*. It seemed that Mexico was a place to make a life for yourself. Nobody was living in fear or isolation, like people in Montreal were at that particular time. People smiled, said hello to their friends, shared food, and didn't avoid eye contact. It looked almost normal, despite having to use masks to enter restaurants and stores. I fell in love with the environment. It was something I needed. Better yet, it got me to reconnect with *mi familia* at Casa Velasco after working hours.

I caught up with *mi tio* Jose, *mi tia* Clarisa, and *mis primos* Hugo, Sara, and Manuel over video calls. Thankfully, I learned Jose managed to keep his restaurant *"Tacquira Velasco"* afloat during the pandemic. Clarisa, a nurse at a local hospital, was able to do some of her office work at home. Hugo, Sara, and Manuel also adapted to the times. It made me feel relieved. After I completed my quarantine period, they all invited me to the house for dinner to reconnect more.

Even before I got to *mi familia's* place in the State of Mexico just outside of *Lomas Tecamalchaco*, I wished that I could have stayed longer. The architecture in the Uber ride was breathtaking, taking me further away from Montreal as I held onto Bellita's notebook in my bag. Maybe it echoed a deeper sense of belonging in my heart when I arrived to find Jose and Clarisa waiting for me at their front door. *Bienvenidos a Mexico*, I thought to myself. Not only did they look the same as they did in 2012, yet their smiles could've lit up all of Mexico if it lost power.

"*Maxito, Maxito, Maxito!*" Jose said, hugging me. "You return! Good to see you, *mi amigo*. But, eh…what happen *contigo*? You gain many kilos by playing less *futbol* and eating more?"

"Hey, *podemos jugar esta noche si quieres!*" I said with a laugh. "I can still outplay you."

"Never!" Jose said, pulling me in tighter. "*Ah, te extraño mucho.* Never go so far again."

"*Claro que si,*" Clarisa said, coming over to kiss my cheek. "We all missed you dearly, like your *tio* has said. Bellita will also be here tonight *con su abuela* and she's so incredibly excited."

"So, how's everyone doing by the way?" I asked them. *Hopefully, no one got sick.*

"Half are *enfermos* and other half are good *en la familia*," Jose said, after a pause. "But in Mexico, we focus on the positives. We know we strong and can thrive. It's how we are, *Maxito*."

After the initial greetings, I entered the house in good spirits. It was then I was reintroduced to Hugo, Sara, and Manuel for the first time since we were teenagers. Now, they were in their twenties with careers. Hugo was an engineer, Sara an interior designer, and Manuel was a partner in Jose's restaurant. Naturally, we reminisced, laughed, and had a good time getting to know each other again. It was great to see them in person rather than on my social media newsfeeds.

Once dinner was on the table, the Spanglish chatter was flowing, the food was perfect, and everyone was comfortable. I told *mi familia* about what it was like to work for a celebrity like Milo. They were curious to know about that lifestyle and I was more than happy to answer.

"Every day is a little different, but essentially I do all the writing you see on Milo's website and social pages," I explained. "So, I'm given tasks by my editors on his team, and it's my job to get that content done before my deadlines, which are usually set for particular times when Milo's audience is the most active online. It's a whole marketing game at the end of the day, *sabes?*"

"Que padre," Manuel said, as Hugo and Sara nodded. "You have got so intelligent."

"Not enough to become the celebrity, however," Jose said, making everyone laugh.

The lighthearted roasting continued until we moved on to the next subject. But when I was in this family dynamic, I also felt sad deep inside. After all, I didn't know how long I'd be in town. It was hard to say if I'd leave Mexico City tomorrow, in a few days, or within a month. Before it affected my mood, though, a voice called out my name. I turned to see it was Bellita.

"Maxito, Maxito!" Bellita said. Her eyes glimmered with joy as she ran and hugged me.

Right then, I almost cried. Despite the time that had passed, Bellita looked the same as she did ten years ago. She wore a dress with printed flowers and had some makeup on. It was obvious Bellita wanted to look her best for me that night. I thought she was the prettiest thing in the world at that moment. But she also didn't lose her enthusiasm. She loved hugs, kisses, high-fives, and dancing. Looking back, she held the rare quality of being "beautiful" inside and out.

"I love to see you," Bellita said, as her *abuela* brought her a chair. "I sit with you, okay?"

"Yes, *claro*! That's more than okay," I said with a smile, which Bellita reciprocated.

"She don't stop talking about you," Bellita's *abuela* said, greeting me with a kiss on the cheek. Everyone called her Abuela Velasco because of her personality, her grace, and her strong will. At the time, she was in her eighties. But since the day Bellita's parents died, she took care of her like a second daughter. I never met another person that selfless. "For a long while, our Bellita keep saying '*mi primo Canadiense viniendo*' over many, many times. I annoyed with her… yet she continue to go on and on and on with no rest. We all miss you, but her the most."

Room was made for Bellita and Abuela Velasco at the dinner table. Our *familia* was complete for the evening. And it was nice to be reunited with *mi prima favorita de* Mexico. Even though Bellita had obstacles because of her disability, she managed to graduate high school. She also found work at *Tacquira Velasco*—making everyone feel welcome as the hostess. She was everyone's best friend. Along with that, I learned Bellita took salsa classes twice a week, had an ex-boyfriend that she met at a special ed math class, and had about 2,000 Facebook friends.

But she didn't use social media obsessively like most people in our generation. If you ask me, Bellita was the definition of being present, which also explained why my little sister, Gabriella, couldn't reach her at times. She was pure in every sense of the word—unlike the two-faced, heartless nature of the corporate world. I would've traded all the virtual meetings with my colleagues for one minute with Bellita at her dance studio. It got me to recognize the significance of what my father said before I left Montreal: Family is what's most important. It's our blood.

"*Entonces, dime como disfrustes Mexico?*" Hugo asked with genuine interest.

"*Mas que puedo explicar,*" I replied. "Honestly, I already want to move here."

"Do this so we can see you way more!" Bellita said. "I know *gente* you can meet *en nuestro restaurante* and we'll dance. We can be together for all the times. And we play games *tambien*."

"Bellita still likes to play Connect Four," Manuel said, adding context. "Everyone is happy when she has breaks, *porque todos saben que los partidos empezando*. It's really so much fun."

"Yes, we have competitions," Jose said. "And I only win *contra* Bellita like four times."

"What you say to Max, *tio*?" Bellita said with a laugh. "You are a cheat. But I know Max not *porque gente* Canadiense are very nice. I read online with my *cellulare* it is so truthful, *no*?"

"Todos en Montreal are nice during the summer," I said to Bellita. "But during winter... *a que veces sí, y a veces no. Depende en la semana,* and the person. But mostly, we're polite."

"Good thing you are here then!" Sara said. "It is warmer and no snow everywhere. But *dime, hablé con Diana y ella le gusta que eres aqui en México.* Apparently, she also work for Milo?"

"Quién es Diana un otra vez?" Bellita asked with a curiosity that was hard to ignore.

"Ah, *si, si,* we called her *el coqueteo grande,*" Hugo said. "In English, *la palabra es...* flirt I think, no?" He turned to everyone for clarification. *"Si,* it is a flirt. I'm certain. Do a favor for you and be careful with this girl. She dates many people at school *y* likes to break their hearts."

"Que cierto porque tengo dos amigos who have date her at the same time without knowing," Manuel said. "And they are no longer friends anymore. She makes them cry, but she smiles."

"Oh, no, no, no," Bellita said, grabbing my arm like I was about to fall from the edge of a mountain. "I recall her because she take *fotos* at salsa class before *la pandemia.* I block her from Facebook because she also dates *mi amigo* Juan at *al restaurante* and breaks up for *un pendejo.*"

"Wait, so Diana cheats like Jose at Connect Four?" I said, making everyone laugh.

"Put it like this—she isn't honorable," Manuel said. "She's for a boy, not for a man."

"I also know she likes to change place a lot," Sara said, *"Después escuela,* we lose touch *porque* she visits many areas in Latino América *y muchas partes de México* in like five years."

"Exactamente!" Bellita said, triumphantly. "She no one to make a life with together."

"Yeah, I know que *tienes razón. Pero, tal vez ella cambió?* Nobody is the same after they're done with school, I mean. Everyone grows up. And maybe, our relationship will be different—"

"What you do for Halloween?" Bellita asked, suddenly. "How long are you in Mexico?"

Looking back, it was a good question. In fact, everyone paused to hear my response.

"Since we just finished quarantine, I don't really know," I replied. "Maybe we'll stay in Mexico City another week or maybe I'll have to leave tomorrow morning? It's up to Milo, to be honest —"

"No, please, don't do it!" Bellita said, cutting me off once more. "You arrive only now. I want to make you know *mis amigos y* show you much more Mexico. Go with us to *el Castillo.*"

"Wait, is there a castle exhibit in Mexico?" I asked, confused. "*Puedes explicar más?*"

"*No, el Castillo de Chapultepec!*"Abuela Velasco said, jumping into the conversation. "That's where her parents first got engaged. It is also history. It was our Prime Minister's home."

"Every year near *Día de los Muertos*, we go out to celebrate their memory," Clarisa said, tearing up a little. "C*on la pandemia* in 2020, we could not enter. But this weekend, we go try."

Right then and there, it occurred to me that I had Bellita's notebook sitting in my bag. I almost completely forgot about it. But thankfully, our dinner conversation reminded me.

"Hey, *sabes que? Traigo un regalo por,* Bellita," I said, catching everyone off guard. "And it's a present from all of us in Canada. Sorry, I didn't bring it up before. But everyone says hi —"

"*Un regalo?!*" Bellita said, turning to *la familia.* "See, I say that *Canadienses* are nice."

The emotions painted on Bellita's face alone made my work trip feel worth the trouble. I walked to the front of the house to find my bag. Bellita and *la familia* followed close behind. And once Bellita saw the notebook, her eyes widened with joy. It was as though I was reuniting her with an old friend. It was like I held a time capsule in my hands able to teleport her to another time. She remembered my mother's English lessons, the person she was as a young girl, her loving parents, and the moment our bond started to grow. She remembered the dreams she had of being able to hold a conversation in the English language. More than that, however, I felt Bellita realized how far she had come in life. Jose, Clarisa, Hugo, Sara, Manuel, and even Abuela Velasco captured everything on their phones. Bellita danced like she won a big award.

"Mi cuaderno en inglés, mi cuaderno en inglés!" Bellita said as she moved around with an energy that was impossible to settle down. "I believe... I thought I would never find this again."

"Well, now you can use it *para siempre!*" I said, opening it to show lots of empty pages.

"I do you poetry tonight," Bellita said with excitement. "Stay here, okay? I come back."

For a while, Bellita was upstairs writing her poems in the bedroom she had at Casa Velasco. Everyone hugged me during the wait. Jose and Clarisa told me it was the sweetest gift I could've given her. *Mis primos* showed me how many likes the video of me handing Bellita the notebook received in the last five minutes. Eventually, Jose had the bright idea of building a little stage for Bellita to read her poetry out loud in the living room. We rearranged the couches to face one direction. Manuel even found a toy microphone for Bellita to use. Everyone thought about someone other than themselves. And it seemed, at least in Casa Velasco, spontaneous moments that were filled with good intentions were a natural thing in everyone's heart. It was endearing.

Once Bellita finished her poems and came running downstairs to see what we made her, she danced with a lot more excitement. It was the same energy whenever she won a game of Connect Four. But before she read her work, my phone rang. I wanted to ignore it, but saw it was Milo. I still recall the pain etched in Bellita's eyes when I answered the call. She almost broke down.

"Where the fuck are you, brother?" Milo said, seemingly in a bad mood. "It's time to go. I'm at the hotel and everyone's packing for Playa Del Carmen. Get your ass back. We need you."

"Can I be over in an hour?" I said, seeing that Jose and Abuela Velasco were trying to comfort her at that moment. "I'm visiting family and I'm being rude. They probably think I—"

"Have to go?" Milo said, cutting me off with little patience. "Well, what the hell did you expect? You're here for me. This isn't a vacation, brother. I pay your salary. I fly you out to dope places for free. I do everything I can to make great music so you can have a job and now we are going to get fucked in Playa. I already have a *Dia de los Muertos* event set up, so get moving."

"It's going to take me a long time to get back, anyway, with the traffic in Mexico alone," I said, pleading my case. "Why can't I just fly out after you guys? I won't be late for the party —"

"No, no, no, just stop!" Milo said. "Check your email, brother. The flight is in six hours."

"But… I'm with my family," I repeated. "I haven't seen them in years. Please, you can at least understand that. This pandemic has been so hard, and reconnecting with family is impor—"

"What about your family with us?" Milo said, cutting me off once again. "That's how things are in case you haven't noticed. That's our culture. It's yours as much as it is mine. And I change my mind a lot. I travel a lot. I party a lot. And I love a lot. Does that make sense, or do I need to find someone to fucking replace you? We do everything together. So… you better be on time."

After that, Milo hung up, and I returned to my seat. I gave Bellita a nice hug, apologized, and reassured her that I wasn't leaving. I told her I would stay for her poems. It put her at ease.

"Today, I come and I see mi primo,
I remember times of our games.
I tell him things and him too.
Maxito speaks in Spanish little
Sometimes also very bad
But he try and I like that he try
Canada es rojo y Mexico has more color
Hope I see Canada since it familia too…"

During that reading, my phone vibrated several times. Along with the email, which held my ticket information, Milo texted me endlessly, asking if I was on the way back. It became stressful. Milo even got a few of my co-workers from editorial to back him up. Bellita was so invested in her poetry that she didn't realize I was distracted. The last half of it was a total blur. In fact, I excused myself to call an Uber ride after she concluded. I was gone in about fifteen minutes. And when I told Bellita I wouldn't be at *el Castillo* with our family, she was devastated.

Chapter 9

November 1, 2021

From the moment I got to Playa Del Carmen around 8:00 a.m. the day before, it became hard to remember an instant when there wasn't a shot of tequila in my hand. Milo took us all clubbing the first night after we got settled into our hotel, introducing us to a rooftop where he played shows in previous years. Naturally, as our team explored the long tourist strip, we kept getting stopped by people who recognized Milo. It was exciting to be sucked into his world of celebrity status like that. But during that particular time, I couldn't believe the madness I saw.

Playa's tourist strip was filled with restaurants, retail stores, street performers, local drug dealers, taxis, and bus drivers. But mostly, there was an endless sea of crowds from numerous parts of the globe. It was overwhelming to realize how much this once sleepy fishing village attracted. It was as though pandemic restrictions no longer existed. I almost forgot there was one.

I met people from Europe, Argentina, Chile, different provinces of Mexico, a few ex-pat Gringos, ex-pat Canadians, and too many other nationalities to count. Everyone was friendly, looking to party, aimlessly walking, and seeking new connections. Having come from Montreal, I was so used to quarantine measures, new variants, curfews, and lockdowns that it seemed hard to imagine a normal world. I forgot what it was like to enjoy life and to be in a destination that encouraged good vibes. Every angle of Playa's tourist strip welcomed the opportunity for fun.

Honestly, it was awkward at first on the rooftop with Milo and our team. But when I got tipsy, blissful energy surged through in a way I hadn't felt since 2019. Milo kept shouting in my ear, *"Mexico para siempre"* like we'd be there for good. He wanted me to feel better about leaving *mi familia* and Bellita behind. He kept selling me on his vision, the brand that gave me a job and purpose during uncertain times. And the worst part is, it worked. I didn't want to go back to Casa Velasco after the great night out we had. He took advantage of my vulnerable state by using the power of celebrity and friendship to make me neglect reality. Even now, I'm disgusted.

The hotel we stayed at was a nice boutique off *Calle 4*, across the street from restaurants, cafes, *lavanderias*, hostels, and convenience stores like Oxxo. It was about fifteen minutes outside the tourist strip. I liked getting work done at a small Italian Café across the street from the hotel, accompanied by digital nomads and little travel groups having breakfast to kick start their day of adventure. But once I'd return, there I'd be with Milo or someone from the team. And with *Dia de los Muertos* coming up, that "party" was the one thing on everyone's mind.

Milo booked a temporary DJ residency at an exclusive club in Playa called "Santino's" for the event. I remember hearing Milo had invested thousands of dollars into making sure it was a memorable night. But for me, that meant one thing: working twelve-hour days writing catchy social media posts, responding to DMs, creating the event page on his website with all the details, and most importantly, writing blog content on "why" Milo chose Santino's. It had to welcome his followers into his mind, to sell them on the experience of Joie Media. They needed to believe they were living as rock stars alongside Milo. It was all a lie, yet that's what Milo prided himself on—beautiful lies and descriptive fantasies which took his brand to new heights.

Looking back now, I was trapped in Milo's fictional version of paradise. The hotel was full of Milo and Joie Media employees. It was like a temporary office. When I returned from the Italian Cafe that November day and worked outside in the common area of our hotel, Milo sat next to me like we were a couple. He flirted by touching my body and complimented my swim trunks. He gave me a drink and offered to buy me dinner for "being his favorite living writer".

Every time I told him to stop, he tried even more to connect. It was a mixed signal I didn't know how to process back then. Milo was making me work extremely hard, yet distracted me like a boyfriend who needed attention, showing his dominance. I got a sudden alpha male vibe that made me fear him a little. Milo abused my time as I tried to maintain his online engagement. But just when I thought it couldn't have gotten worse, Milo brought up his costume suggestion.

"What do you think, brother? I want your opinion," Milo said, showing me a photo of a couple wearing traditional clothes and skeleton makeup as if they were royalty in the afterlife.

"I'm not sure, to be honest," I replied, after a pause. "But they look great together... Is this in Oaxaca or something? I remember my cousins saying once the best parties for Dia de los —"

Milo cut me off by placing a finger to my mouth. "I already ordered those exact costumes, and the makeup people will be here later tomorrow." He then placed his other hand on my lap firmly. It was as though Milo wanted me to realize I wasn't in control of anything. It was a fire, an energy, a side of him I never experienced. But one thing's for sure: I was afraid to say no to him at that moment. "We're partners, brother. You're my employee...my greatest one. And we're going to kill it tomorrow, Montreal style. It'll be just like our soccer days, but even better."

"Yeah, but before that happens, I need to call *mi familia* to wish them a happy *Dia de los Muertos*," I said, getting out of my seat and preparing to go to my room. "I know my cousin—"

"Whatever, just get it done!" It was clear by his abruptness he lacked interest in that part of my life. "I bet you they don't even care that you're gone. It's not like you're always there."

"How the fuck do you know?" It was like a switch went off and all I saw was red.

Suddenly, Milo got out of his seat and came up to my face. I noticed that people from our team watched from a distance, wondering how it'd all play out. It felt embarrassing in retrospect.

"No one will ever, *ever* love you like I do," Milo said with a smile and mad look in his eyes. "Remember that, okay? I know you for who you really are. I know secrets your family may never find out about you, so we're linked. Nobody will get your experiences like me, or people just like me, if you get what I'm saying, brother. If that's not love, then I don't know what is!"

Politely, I just nodded. But deep down, I was furious at him for not caring about how I disappointed Bellita and *mi familia*. It was upsetting that he questioned my love for the people in my life. There was never a free moment to video chat with them since we got to Playa. I worked too much and partied even harder in less than forty-eight hours. Milo was happy when I nodded, however. And since there wasn't any work left to do, I asked Milo if I could walk on the beach.

"Yes, sure… anything for you to be happy," Milo said. "But know that I'm letting you."

"Can I go or not, though?" I asked, confused by the point he was trying to make.

"Sorry if I'm acting weird," Milo said, rubbing my lower back. "It just brings me lots of joy to picture you as a hot skeleton. In fact… it just makes me feel a certain way, if you get that."

"Well… it'll be a great party tomorrow," I said. I felt him staring at me as I left the hotel.

Between Mexico City and Playa, the only alone time I had was the walk on the beach. I left my towel, my flip-flops, my Gatsby novel, and even my phone behind to signify a landmark. The sand felt nice as my feet sunk deep into it. The clouds in the sky made me smile, reminding me of artwork at a museum. It helped to clear my head from all the screen time I needed to endure. Suddenly, feeling liberated, the ocean beckoned me to swim within it until I reached Cozumel.

Walking along the beach's shores, my mind wandered to the unfulfilled promises of "life after graduation". I really thought I'd be a journalist working for a popular media outlet, writing about the pandemic, and making a difference in the world. But instead, I wrote clickbait and social media content for Milo's brand. I remember asking God what my "next move" should be while passing neighboring hotels, families, groups of people speaking different languages, and a few local street dogs. It was at that moment I decided I'd send my resume to other employers. I needed to rediscover the same peace I did when I saw everyone at Casa Velasco. Maybe being in Playa was enough? But the more I walked endlessly, the more my questions went unanswered.

Quietly, it was clear to me I had enough knowledge and experience to land a job somewhere else. It's what also convinced me to write short stories about the "grand adventures working for a celebrity in 2021". I began feeding this creative energy later that month, submitting pieces to literary journals and digital magazines with reckless abandon. Looking back on this, the writing could have been more refined. After all, I'd finish my stories and send them off within the hour Joie Media gave me for lunch—dreaming one of them would get published by someone. But the querying process was daunting. Suddenly, as I waited to be discovered, the idea of working forever with Milo crept into my head. It felt depressing in a way I could never explain.

"Please, lord, *Dios, universo…* C'mon, there's got to be somebody out there in Montreal, Toronto, the US, or even Europe that'll be interested in hiring me, right?" I mumbled, alone on the beach, heading back toward where I left my towel. "I know I have the talent to wow people. And I know that I'd thrive without Milo. Please, just give me a sign. God, you know I need something. And it needs to be something good. Something now. Please…tell me I'm not crazy."

My arms stretched toward the sky, as though I was challenging the Mayans who painted the clouds above to give me an answer to my questions. But I also thought of the "stories" that I wanted to send out to publishers. Despite the fact journalism was my major, I always dreamed of becoming a novelist. Collecting my things, I figured there was no harm in trying to become one.

Funny enough, I also considered working for a popular sports network, teaching English as a second language abroad, backpacking through Europe for a year, becoming a master chef (eating out in Mexico can inspire that course of action), or inventing a time machine to stop myself from agreeing to work for Milo. But while my mind raced, a moment of distraction occurred. From a slight distance, there was Diana on the beach. I recognized her because of her photos and reels on Instagram. I also knew she'd be in Playa for Milo's event. I thought Diana was still in Tulum, working her magic as a social media manager and digital nomad influencer. But in that brief instant, Diana was prettier and far more captivating than talking with her on my laptop.

Nervous as I tried to play it cool, I spotted the cute bracelet on her right ankle, her tanned skin that'd make Mayan Gods jealous, her blondish streaks that complimented her brown hair, the sunglasses on her face, and the creative energy she possessed with the vintage camera hanging from her neck. I was drawn to how Diana carried herself. She had a presence. It was the kind of quality of intrigue social media could never provide. No, it was a real spark that made me at a loss for words. I felt desperate to start a conversation with her, yet I didn't have the guts.

Diana was my type from an initial standpoint: beautiful, artistic, a little mysterious, graceful, intelligent, and mesmerizing with every second that passed me by. Being invested in Milo's company perhaps was meant to be so that I would cross paths with that *bonita mujer*. On the beaches of Playa, all I saw was Diana Romero—captivating the galaxy with an everlasting light.

Even with that fantasy in mind, however, Milo's word from earlier popped into my head. Is it possible I'd never find genuine love with Diana, or anyone else for that matter? Would I ever be brave enough to tell her my big secrets? Reflecting on this now, it might have saved me a lot of heartache if Diana knew the story of my ultimate truth. But I didn't want to ruin the potential for a romance of the ages. I didn't have control over my emotions. And that was my own fault.

Honestly, I didn't know why Diana's presence impacted me without much effort. But one thing's for sure: I wanted to connect with her deeply at Milo's event. She was my *Playa Crush*.

Chapter 10

November 2, 2021

Milo was being promoted on social media as Santino's headliner for *Dia de los Muertos*—a popular club in the heart of Calle 8, where Playa came alive in the evening with the buzzing of tourists and local characters. I saw groups of people wearing traditional outfits and wearing skeleton makeup with pride. They danced wildly, bringing forth a positive energy that brought a natural smile to your face. What touched my heart the most, though, was seeing all the families who came together to honor their past loved ones, carrying gifts and food to honor their name.

Before the event kicked off, Milo was clear that he wanted to make a statement. It was a job requirement to have a good time for the video team to capture for Insta reels, TikTok, and ultimately a promotional clip to market his third album. He planned to surprise everyone at Santino's with new singles that were set to be released later in the year. The way Milo put it: this would be how he showed the pandemic made him stronger. Most of the Joie Media team drank like their lives depended on it. But I felt suffocated. Leading up to things, a lot was on my mind.

Each restaurant on the tourist strip was covered with *Dia de los Muertos* decorations, with street performers putting on shows that featured epic dances. Vendors offered tequila and mezcal more excitedly than before, and DJs played loudly from every club with an energy level you could only feel if you were there that night. Playa wasn't shy to illustrate the magic in the air for people to experience, making a true statement to the underworld that the dead were being celebrated. Milo's DJ set, in particular, was rhythmic, full of a vibrancy that drew people closer to the booth where he played. It got so crazy that his fans wanted to climb up to shake his hand and take photos for their social media pages. If it wasn't for the security guards, Milo would've gotten trampled with love. But Milo allowed some fans to join him on his little stage—giving them a chance to enjoy the madness of "choosing life over pain" as Milo continued to define it.

Drunk and careless, Milo yelled into his microphone at one point that the best cure for prolonged isolation was to "dance it off". Everyone cheered and followed his lead—worshiping him like a God. None of the public health measures were being respected. There was no mask in sight unless it was part of a costume. It would've driven everyone back in Montreal insane if they saw what was happening, my parents included. But while I stood dressed as a skeleton—coordinated by Milo for everyone to see in an Instagram photo just before the Santino's event—I didn't have a second to myself to call *mi familia* at Casa Velasco. Everyone wanted to drink with me, to take photos since I was "trending everywhere online". The Joie Media videographers captured footage of me at Santino's when I consumed tequila shots, socialized, and danced to Milo's big drops. Certain parts of the night were admittedly fun. But there was also the sense of being judged by Milo's fans, especially when they'd approach me to compliment my outfit.

Many assumed I was Milo's "boyfriend". Some people even brought up that we made a great couple. Despite it all, though, there was another reason everyone believed it was true. The night before, I had convinced Milo to go along with me on a day trip to Chichen Itza—originally the home of *los Mayas*, one of the nine wonders on earth, a slice of history I found intriguing.

The truth behind escaping to Chichen Itza during the day was not to see Diana until the event. Looking back, my rationale was much too idealized. But I didn't want Diana's first impression of me to be in our hotel's common area hunched over my laptop. Gone all day until the evening, Diana would see me at my best. She viewed my Instagram stories during that day trip, fueling the anticipation of our first official meeting in my head. Honestly, I've got no regrets because there was no chance Milo would've let me go unless I invited him. Maybe I used Milo's love for me to my advantage. But what I experienced at Chichen Itza made things worthwhile.

Milo perceived it as a date—taking photos for social media attention, shooting TikToks of us walking, and saying things while he filmed like *"feel good vibes with the greatest man"*. Suddenly, I noticed Milo was getting attached to the idea of us being a couple, especially when others encouraged it. Honestly, the fans contributed to the problems I had. Even my co-workers at the party couldn't stop talking about how romantic it was for me to take Milo on a "dream-like adventure". It was the office gossip. But it didn't matter because I loved my visit to Chichen Itza.

* * * *

Chichen Itza looked so well preserved that it seemed like you were frozen in time. The impression of the ruins was that the Mayan culture, art, and beauty were things that can never be forgotten. The architecture and proof of civilization beyond our modern understanding appeared like it would never vanish. It stared at you with confidence from the pyramid-like structures with a million soaring clouds above the blue sky, as if the people who lived in that lost time were present somehow. I knew there was nothing else like it back home in Montreal. But it was the Mayan horoscope reading I got that piqued my interest most. It turned out I was a *Falcon*—the sign blessed with good luck, and a defined personality and character dating to my youth. They're also considered to be strong individuals, responsible adults, and intellectual beings. I didn't believe the "intellectual" part, though. Besides, during the long bus ride over, when Milo had fallen asleep, I checked my phone to find two job rejection emails and four magazine rejections.

Both companies liked my resume yet didn't want to give me a fair chance. In the same regard, the magazine people rejected my stories, but also expressed how much they loved my writing style and encouraged me to submit more often. Maybe, if I wasn't in Chichen Itza and got the disappointing news while being stressed out in my remote office space, it would have led to depression. But the highlight of my day trip was reading the Falcon's perspective on "love".

Not only is a Falcon man infatuated by the aura of beautiful people, but he's also destined to have one great love forever engraved in his heart. Even if the Falcon male ends up marrying a few times in life, a part of him will always be saved for that one special person. The funny thing is my mind immediately went to my Gatsby novel. Maybe I was Jay in the story of my world—giving up everything for my shot at one idealized type of happiness, even if I can have many others just as fulfilling. But yet, who was my Daisy? It seemed that it was Milo to everyone at the *Dia de los Muertos* event. He pulled me into his DJ booth whenever one of his new singles came flowing into the playlist. It's crazy how Milo thought I liked him as much as he did. And because I didn't want to lose my job at that point in time, I complied with his fantasy of "us".

"I'm so happy beyond words that I hired you, brother!" Milo said, while a handful of our team was hanging out in the DJ booth. It was big enough to fit about five people. "You work so hard, produce such great content, and make us look amazing. Everybody on the team loves you."

"Thanks," I said, separating myself from his body. "Hopefully, I'll be here a while—"

"Hey, everyone, isn't Max our employee of the year?" Milo yelled into his microphone as people on the dance floor cheered. "We should give him a trophy. Fuck, maybe even a raise!"

"Oh, I can totally make that happen," Peter from the accounting department said. He sent me an automated "Congrats" on LinkedIn the day I got hired, but we haven't really talked since.

"Max is the fucking man!" Jennifer said, catching me off guard since I was used to more constructive feedback from her than anything positive. I just smiled and politely raised my drink.

"Reach out anytime," Daniel said, although he continued to ghost me after that night and gave me these weird, passive grins if we crossed paths at the hotel. "I'd love to give you advice."

"Yes, I second that!" Nate said, another copywriter. "My door is always open." But it never was. He saw me more as the competition as opposed to a teammate. He never *DM'd* me online.

"See, brother," Milo said. "There's no need to worry about staying or going. We're all here to support you while you grow. It's all really genuine, brother. You should realize that by now."

"Hopefully, you'll stay with us for years," Francois from the video production team said.

Everyone raised their glasses to that, while Milo pulled me close once again with sudden aggression. It was evident Milo became violent the more he drank. My chances of escaping were slim to none. But I got lucky once the party went past eleven p.m. Since I missed a day of work to see Chichen Itza with Milo, I needed to make up for it early the next morning. It was reasonable when I called it and headed back to the hotel. Nobody thought that it was strange.

Twenty minutes later, I stumbled to the hotel's corridor with nothing in mind except my bed. I had to walk past the front gate where the common area was located, take a sharp right just before the information booth, and then go up the stairs until I got to my room. Predictably, I felt disoriented and upbeat thanks to the many tequila shots. I wasn't looking my best either since I was tired from the day I had. But then, a bright laptop light came into view. Near the information booth, there was Diana—my *Playa Crush*. It was the first time I found myself around her without the distraction of others. Looking back, it was a golden opportunity at something perfect.

"*Hola*, Diana… What's up?" I said, awkwardly. "*Sabes…* do you know who I am?"

Taken by surprise, Diana turned my way. Her brown eyes glittered in a way I won't forget. She looked at me with a smile and curiosity in her heart that touched mine. Her expression revealed she knew who I was. Even though it was late, I got the feeling Diana was up for a little adventure with someone that intrigued her enough to stop working. I wasn't aware of this back then. But now, I know spontaneous action was Diana's life philosophy on that night and others to come. A lot would happen before anyone could even read her thoughts. She was a true mystery, yet I loved that about her. It felt like Diana had secrets and couldn't decide whether to share them or not. More importantly, you needed to be special for Diana to express herself to you.

"Que gusto verte, finalmente!" Diana said, getting out of her seat to kiss my cheek and offered a hug that made me shake on the inside. It was full of love and kindness, which was the opposite of Milo's aggression. "You don't understand. I try million times to say hi, *pero yo vi que estabas siempre* busy with things. I don't come near since you work. But I say hello now."

"Creo que tenemos ahorita un momento perfecto por una hola," I said, continuing to feel her warmth. "I did see you take pics *en la playa*, though. But I didn't want to disturb you either."

Before too long, a range of emotions alternated on Diana's face that even the greatest mind reader on earth couldn't decipher. It's something I would've never known through a video call or text message. The pandemic had made me forget what it was like to meet someone in real life for the very first time. The experience was so pure and wonderful that I hoped it would never end.

"Que guapo eres tú as a skeleton*!"* Diana said, playfully analyzing my costume.

"*Si,* and now I'm here to save you from boredom," I said, making her laugh. *"Pero, dimelo, porqué no estas en Santino's con todos en el negocio?* Honestly, I wanted to say hi to you there."

"I'm happy you speaking in Spanish for real," Diana said. "I didn't expect this before. I know you are not from Mexico, so I believe at times you use a translator. I'm glad it's not true."

"No, well... *uso y no uso,*" I said, blushing. "*Depende, honestamente.* See, I know how to order food, ask for directions, and verbs. But I'm not fluent yet. Hopefully one day, though."

"It's really fine, *tu* Spanglish *es perfecto conmigo,*" Diana said with affection in her voice. "It better than drunk Americans. Even though you pass as one, you're way different and cute."

"Good thing you're with un *Canadiense* then," I said. "We're a lot nicer than they are."

"That's the reason I don't go tonight," Diana said with another laugh that captivated me even more. "No one interests me here, *y hablé con* most people there before. I decide *necesité un noche solamente para mi, entiendes?* But Wi-Fi here is better than in my room. So, I'm outside."

"Well, if you ask me, I feel like your night is better than mine," I said, unable to believe I overshared with her like that. "It was fun while I was there but...but I-I left for similar reasons."

Right then, Diana looked at me with concern. In a quiet way, she wanted to help me feel better. I got that impression when she reached for my hands. And once I gripped hers back, I felt electricity shoot through my body. It was like her affection took away the pain I felt on a deep subconscious level. She was genuine, engaging, and offered her presence. Strangely, I felt relaxed. It seemed like the beginning of me falling for my *Playa Crush.* After all, a night full of possibility and a little empty hotel lobby appeared to be the perfect equation for magic to happen.

"*No te preocupes,*" Diana said. "It is good to enjoy *fiestas* before reality come again."

"Don't remind me, please," I said, feeling my palms begin to sweat. "It's funny how going to parties is supposed to help you forget about your problems, but I now just seem to be thinking about them more *a huevo.* I'm trying to have a good time, yet I feel it's hard for me to do that."

"Maybe the bad problems need to be resolve before you start enjoying again?" Diana said with compassion. "This is good, *amigo*. You will be happier once you solve these challenges."

"God, that just makes me want to drink more tequila."

Even though I came off as pessimistic, Diana wasn't fazed by it. She reassured me everything was okay. The innocent spark we created together developed into something full of excitement. It felt easy, natural, and peaceful to a great extent. On my end, it was refreshing not to be judged for being Milo's friend, my work ethic, my performance, and other annoyances. I was free during my conversation with Diana—we were one. Better yet, there was something about her body language that ignited butterflies in my stomach. Milo and my "career" didn't matter anymore. Diana cast her spell. I was hooked. And who knew what was in store tonight?

"So, anyway... *que* photos are you editing?" I asked, breaking the tension I created.

"Nada." Diana showed me her laptop. "Look, I take of *familias,* the birds, *y del mar*."

Quickly surveying her work, it was evident Diana had talent. The way she played around with the lighting, her camera angles, and her subjects correlated together in unison. I felt the energy of the *familias* she captured; the birds flying high in the sky, and the ocean's heart. Diana wasn't just creative—she was a real artist. I saw Diana's fingerprints in everything that she did.

"Honestly, I love them," I said with heartfelt sincerity. "And I can relate to your process."

"Oh, it's true for you?" Diana said, intrigued. Reflecting on it now, I don't know how she kept me in a trance with every word—even in her broken, imperfect English. I was sold forever.

"Yes... I do more than write for Milo. I also work on my own stories, so I edit a lot too."

Right then, Diana's brown eyes widened with excitement. That caught her attention. It was the first time I ever felt comfortable telling someone I wanted to become a novelist. And the spark in her eyes bizarrely made me feel confident in my hope of getting stories published. She made me believe it was possible. Even now, I never let go of that acceptance long after Mexico.

"That's interesting, *mi amigo Canadiense*," Diana said. "How great that you have such a heart like this! I wouldn't guess before you like stories and arts, and stuff like that, but I love it."

"Maybe I don't look the part. But *sabes algo....* I want to sell my work to publishers. "

"Art is not for money," Diana said with a blank expression. "It is for the soul, always."

"Yeah, I get that completely—"

"Have you gone to *Europa, amigo*?" Diana said. You felt the anticipation in her tone.

"Nunca en mi vida," I said. "But I don't know, maybe someday? It's on my bucket list."

"Go," Diana said. "It's only then you see all the poetry and architecture and theater and cities that have been around for long times. I can't even count how much. No more are the ones who made it here anymore, but their art lives on. Money can't buy such achievements, *no*? Art is about shaping and creating worlds, not being rich. If you move the people, then that is enough."

"Hopefully I'll go soon if I get vacation days because I've always wanted to explore the cities of Europe," I said. "But for now... I'm stuck here. In fact, I doubt I'm going anywhere."

Suddenly, Diana smiled with a grace filled with mysterious affection. It was impossible to know what was on her mind. But once Diana smiled, her face portrayed more emotion than anything I'd ever seen. It appeared like I'd been lost in Diana's world for an eternity, despite the fact we only chatted for ten minutes. But then, I realized I didn't need to know—I had to let go, trusting Diana had nothing other than good energy to share. It felt comforting knowing she was a beautiful woman in my life, a friend I didn't just talk to online. A part of me didn't want her smile to dissipate. But disrupting that entire fantasy, she turned off her laptop and began to walk.

"Hey, hey, *a dónde vamos?*" I asked, taken by surprise when she grabbed my hand and rushed toward our hotel's front gate. "It's getting really late and... I-I can't stay out too long—"

"Be patient and open to things, *amigo*," Diana said. "Allow *esta noche* to engage you."

"Fine, I... *tengo un mente abierto?*" I said, after a pause. "I'm an open book."

"Orale, va!" Diana said, pulling me with a spirit for adventure. "Tonight, we go and live."

Chapter 11

November 3, 2021

Faster than I could've expected, Diana led me past the hotel until we reached the tourist strip. Her enthusiasm didn't waiver as she dragged me along in the opposite direction of all the *Día de los Muertos* festivities. I remember walking until we got to Calle 1, on the beach next to the ferry station, which took you to the Island of Cozumel. It was quieter in the evening since the ferry and the shops nearby were closed. It felt intimate, almost like we had stepped into the part of our story where we realized this encounter was meant to be true. But as that idea spiraled in my head, Diana turned with a smile before leading us onto the sand—where nobody else was in sight, where the night was pure as though *los Mayas* always knew we'd be there, where I saw nothing but tides and my *Playa Crush*. I don't know how my heart didn't beat out of my chest.

Calmly, Diana and I strolled on the empty beach until we picked a comfortable spot to sit down. Our guide was the moonlight that set the mood perfectly. Despite the echoes of music sounding from *Día de los Muertos*, the world appeared nonexistent—placing us in a meditative state. Even though my curiosity was piqued, I waited for her to reveal the purpose of all this.

Diana seemed to appreciate my quiet nature, engaged in our little adventure with the bliss and wonder of a young child. It was the kind of moment that made me realize the value of books, artwork, and poetry. It made me understand stories were meaningful, yet one had to live first to tell them right. Every talented novelist I knew had one big thing in common—they wrote about universal themes capable of getting readers to experience how they once felt. It's an exchange of words that hopes to inspire one to see their own potential greatness in the world. And when I sat there with Diana, I felt she would guide me toward the light of each beautiful memory to come.

The ocean also echoed a type of peace that felt nostalgic to my experience at Chichen Itza—history reflected at me on the same waters *los Mayas* saw centuries ago. Strangely, it got Diana and I to see the promises of tomorrow made yesterday. Goosebumps rose when Diana got closer, placing her head on my shoulder like it was a pillow. *Maybe*, I thought, *we were now alone in the universe.* But as the ocean reminded me of the many stories it carried, the more I saw the importance of my own. With Diana leaning against me, I also realized "love" is a universal theme for good reason. It's what we long for and what we secretly want. It's not the fancy office job, work culture, or even a high salary, but knowing somebody on earth has got your back.

Suddenly, I gained the confidence to believe I'd find another job. I believed I'd find the right publisher. It was a truth I prayed for as of late. And it was then Diana opened up about hers.

"Years ago, when I leave from school to be a photographer, I worked as a lifeguard in Cancun," Diana said with a fond recollection. "I liked it a lot, it was so cool. But *a lo mejor*, I would...I would, you know, look at the people having great times and it would make me sad. I wanted to be *con ellos*. I wanted to be with the people at the resorts. I take the photos, at first, *por divertido y* Instagram. But as I explored the art of photography more, I knew I had been doing what I should. I look at the people, watch them smile at me, and I feel like I do good things. Near *las playas*, enjoying, feeling sand *en mis pies*, and being glad with the cameras. I take photos *de los niños* with mothers, I capture people *vacaciones*, and other beauties. That is my passion *en la vida y me encanta*. Maybe they see me for a day, but I see them for all times."

"So, is that why you're a social media manager now?" I asked her out of curiosity.

"I don't see it as such," Diana said, looking at me with fire in her eyes. "The world has change, *entiendes*, and today *encontramos* photos *en muchas formas en internet*. So, I work on my passions. And I'm good because I do with love and care. It is, as they say, a calling for me."

"That's something I can't deny," I said, feeling so drawn to her energy that I found myself getting a little closer to her on the beach. "After all... I can see you like photos *mas que fiestas*."

"*Como te dije*, I commit to my loves," Diana said, turning to me with a dreamy gaze. "And this love *que tengo es por todos mis fotos*, videos, *y gente* that forever inspire me to do my art."

"Damn, that's a beautiful mindset if I ever heard one," I said, blown away by her sweet approach to things. "It just makes me wonder how many *lugares* are represented in your photos."

"Yes, it is vast *como al mar en frente*," Diana said with a perpetuating excitement. "And when you see it where you are, it's nice to see it can lead anywhere. I look before you go near Chichen Itza *con* Milo, *verdad*? I love when I go visit there. And the geography *los Mayas* discovered amaze me. If you travel in one way in the ocean, you'll be in Cuba. Another goes to Puerto Rico. And another to Miami. I want to go everywhere. And I know I can. Someday, I will take photos of everywhere. I will experience my life *con mis amigos en todas partes del mundo*."

Speechless by the hypnotizing visions of Diana's dreams, I listened attentively until she no longer had another thought to share. For a minute or two, I thought I was teleported into another realm belonging only to me and my *Playa Crush*. I was now a part of her grand vision for life. But either way, I felt that I needed to add something immense to feed into our brief moment. I didn't want it to end yet. I wanted the still Playa night to remain always present in our hearts.

"Honestly, it sounds like you've got it figured out!" I said, breaking the silence like a wave caressing the shore. "It's because, you know...I feel like people, nowadays, are more interested in taking photos and wasting time watching others live through a screen. I'm not complaining since it's the reason I have a job. It's the reason I'm here with you now, actually. But I feel people don't know how to enjoy stuff anymore without also trying to document everything. I don't know… perhaps I'm an old soul. Or maybe I'm burning out. Anyway, in case I'm not making sense, I love your perspective because you're really living life. You're embracing the world to a degree I'm struggling with lately. So, maybe… maybe I'll join you on your travels."

"More and the merrier, like *todo los Gringos* are saying," Diana said, inciting banter. "But, *dimelo*, what about you? *Hablo mucho, pero tu no hablas*. Why you do writing? I am curious."

For a while, I considered the question. Nobody had asked me something that personal in a long time. But it was done with such raw tenderness that it was quite frightening. I knew I could have run past Diana as she worked in the information booth. I knew I could have stayed at Milo's event. But instead, there I was, romantically enthralled with Diana. It seemed now I found myself in a movie-like scene I wouldn't have traded for anything. It wasn't an exaggeration—I forgot for a minute that I had my job. No longer did I have responsibilities in Playa Del Carmen.

"Maybe it's because it gives me hope and reassurance when I've got nothing left?" I said, while Diana patiently stared at me with interest. "I don't know… Does that make any sense?"

"Siempre puedes hablar conmigo," Diana replied. It almost made me shiver with tears. Her intent was pure, and endearing based on the sound of her voice. And I couldn't tell if a kiss on her lips would ruin things or take it to the next level. Right then, Diana became part of my life in a special way I couldn't have ever imagined. It made me believe perhaps everything was looking up for the better. I was falling apart mentally, while also being pieced back together. I felt myself grow the longer I stayed with Diana—or, at the least, I knew the potential was there.

"You inspired me tonight, so I'd be down to talk more," I said. "Well, I know we message each other on *Insta* a lot and we also work for Milo, but…I-I like this. I like this right now."

"Me too, amigo," Diana said, slowly getting up. *"Vamos,* I am tired. It is late and we need our rests. Maybe I see you walking tomorrow. I don't know how, but I'll be very excited if I do."

When I got back to my hotel room, it was 12:45 a.m. and there was this acute wondering that lingered in my heart. If I saw Diana the next day, would we be able to replicate every ounce of hope we captured on that beautiful night? Or, more accurately, would I continue to be stranded in Mexico hoping to move toward a new chapter—"professional triumph", as defined by my Falcon sign. Was I already in love with her? Either way, I began to draft a short story on everything that happened, to preserve each memory we created together. I began to see how one person could really be enough to comfort you when things were hard. I felt rejuvenated. But disrupting that nice image, I got a drunk text message from Milo. It came with a half-nude photo.

"Thinkin' about you, brother." The caption read. "Come to my room wheneverrrr."

Chapter 12

November 29, 2021

Waking up that morning wasn't different from any other morning that followed the last month. On my phone, there were missed video calls from my parents with texts urging me to call them back. I read news articles sent to me online by friends who knew I wasn't in Montreal. But mostly, I experienced the guilt of knowing I was happy to be isolated from their pandemic issues.

Back home, the news reported thousands of positive cases in Quebec during the fourth wave of the pandemic—leading to countless lockdowns and healthcare measures in place once the summer ended. Restaurants, schools, malls, movie theatres, businesses, cafes, and many other establishments remained closed. Friends on social media complained about music festivals and other wonderful events that were canceled in Montreal. Everyone continued to stay home, work from home, and do everything else at home unless something like groceries were needed. Nothing had really changed since the day Milo brought me to Mexico. And even though most Canadians were double vaccinated at that point, it still wasn't enough for hope to be restored.

Strangely, I found every COVID-19-related article did a phenomenal job of depicting the world as an apocalyptic-type universe. It was a message that rippled into the fears of people on social media, and later into frustration due to the broken promises made on a political level. No one in Montreal wanted another lockdown to happen. Nobody wanted to be unable to head to their favorite restaurants, or their local gym, or be unemployed. Nobody wanted to be depressed.

What was next? Global alien invasions? It was funny, yet terrifying to imagine the world's fate as it was beginning to crumble into millions of pieces. Honestly, just like everyone else, I would've never expected something like the pandemic to happen in my lifetime. Never did I imagine I'd struggle to maintain hope that it would end before too long. But like the expat artists and writers of 1920s Paris, I wanted to believe there'd be a roaring new start to life once the COVID-19 era would be a thing of the past. I wanted to believe good things were to come.

Despite my everlasting optimism, though, the bitter realities of the pandemic also made it hard for Milo to post daily content for a while. The Instagram live video he shot for *Día de los Muertos* received backlash from his fans in Canada, the United States, Europe, and parts of Latin America. It got so bad that it even forced him to post an official apology. Luckily, the singles he played at the event were viral hits on TikTok. We spent time creating blogs highlighting the meaning behind the songs Milo played from his third album. But overall, the workflow at Joie Media was not as fast-paced. In fact, it became stagnant as Milo waited for the heat to cool off.

Coincidentally, a bunch of Milo's celebrity friends also got in major trouble for hosting parties, shooting movies, breaking public health rules, writing questionable social posts, and the list goes on. And quite like Milo, they needed to post apologies to follow their careless behavior. The potential for backlash, heat, and notoriety for expressing views and "good vibes" (as Milo called it) seemed outlawed—especially if it came from someone experiencing a level of comfort 99.9% of people would never have. Milo, by default, was an easy target for angry people online.

Over the last month, we also reshared popular content, repackaged snippets from Milo's new songs, and posted the Instagram photos and blogs we didn't have time to do. It was enough to keep us a little busy, yet not enough to distract us from the growing concern of making it back to our respective countries. Nobody wanted to go through the headache of returning to Canada, for example, after our 180-day Mexican tourist visas expired. Most of us felt restless and wanted to be with our families. Some argued they didn't want to return until the pandemic was over—digital nomad life suited their personal needs. But when these issues surfaced, Milo called a breakfast meeting that late November. Everyone hoped it would solve our unanswered questions.

Meanwhile, since I had a lot of free time in November, my whole life centered on refreshing job sites, writing bad short stories, and reassuring everyone in Montreal that *la familia* in Mexico was safe. But in retrospect, it was dedicated more to exploring the romance I wanted to create with Diana. When I got to a French place called *Chez Celine* for the meeting— Milo's favorite restaurant in Playa and a global culinary hit he bought out that morning—it came to the point where I couldn't stop refreshing my Instagram feed to check if she replied to my messages.

But it didn't take long to figure out that Diana was an enigma. Honestly, there were days when I'd see her on the beach and in various restaurants, bars, and clubs in Playa Del Carmen. I'd even see her walking around with friends. I'd say hello and join in on the fun. But there were also days when Diana would disappear and refuse to be found. She'd go as far as being inactive online. There was no in-between. And when I didn't see her at Milo's meeting, it was the latter.

Right when everyone at Joie Media got to the restaurant, I searched for Diana. I looked at members of my team spread across four different tables, hoping I'd see her face. Every minute I'd check my phone to see if she posted anything new online. Whenever I heard laughter or a tone of voice that reminded me of her, I'd turn to see if my *Playa Crush* was anywhere in sight.

For a moment or two, I also considered the possibility Diana was on the beach gathering material. I didn't know why Diana chose to vanish on that November morning. It was so bizarre that I feared the absolute worst. Maybe she woke up with a terrible fever? While I ate my breakfast and made small talk with people around me, there were hundreds of scenarios that ran through my mind. But somewhere in between, I recall getting a startling text from my mother.

"Someone in the family might've tested positive for covid. Please, give me a call."

I'll never forget how that brief message struck me on a psychological level. Suddenly, the pandemic became a part of the world I knew. It wasn't just something I read about online anymore. Now, I became part of the narrative of those who got infected. Before I called my mother, I skimmed through the day's pandemic-related news articles with a more careful eye. I reviewed the facts and prayed the death count wasn't so bad. The emotions were overwhelming.

"I don't know if you've heard, but your Uncle Jose is coughing a lot," my mother said when I called her just outside Chez Celine. "He also has trouble breathing, and now others in the house could get sick. Did you check up on them? Do you know what happened? We're scared."

For a minute, there wasn't much that could've been said. It was suddenly difficult for me to breath. Better yet, I realized what poor a job I'd done staying in touch with *mi familia*. Since the day I left Mexico City and Casa Velasco behind, it seemed there was no connection between me and that part of my identity anymore. It felt like I was back in quarantine all over, isolated from everyone I loved most. My hands began to shake while I held onto my phone with that idea in mind. But yet, I also wanted to reassure my mother and family back home. So, I decided to lie.

"Yeah, well, I talked to Jose and Clarisa about two weeks ago. It seemed like things were fine, but who knows… Maybe I'll call them later tonight or something and give you an update."

"That would be amazing, thank you!" my mother said. "But I'm especially worried about Bellita. I'm sure you know, but it was Manuel's birthday three weeks ago, and there was a *fiesta* at the *taqueria*. Gabriella told me that it was packed. I saw all the photos and the videos online."

"Oh, I... I might've been working late because I don't recall seeing that," I said, feeling my heart shatter a little bit. How could I have forgotten Manuel's birthday in early November? I couldn't believe I scrolled past all the photos. Playa Del Carmen was overpowering my world.

"Did you at least wish Manuel a happy birthday on Facebook?" my mother asked.

"Why wouldn't I have—" Yet another lie.

"Good, because we need to be there for our family," my mother sharply replied. "Even if we're busy in life, it's the most important thing. God, I'm praying that someone didn't infect Bellita at Manuel's *fiesta*. I hope that she's okay because you know how she can be at parties."

"She's the life of them," I said, hearing my mother's voice choking back tears. It was a lost cause trying to find the right words to comfort her. The best thing would be to call Jose after my work meeting. Nothing poetic could've solved this—words that lack action often lose their meaning. I had to focus on the little things, the small victories, and steps in the right direction. I wanted to believe things were and always would be good. That's what Bellita deserved.

"Don't worry, Mom, I'll call Jose after we hang up," I said. "And I'll update you with all the details. Jose's strong and full of heart. He'll be okay, I promise. Everyone else will be too."

"All we need to know is if he's covid positive or not," my mother said. "Please, call us the second you know. Since the *fiesta*, people in our family and others who were at the house got sick. You know them, Max, they always see each other. So, if Jose tested positive for covid, there's a good chance Bellita might have too, and I...I can't imagine what'll happen if she does."

"I'll find out everything," I said reassuringly. "It's all going to work out, you'll see..."

Suddenly, Milo walked into the restaurant and quickly demanded everyone's attention.

"Are you busy?" my mother asked, noticing the awkward pause on my end of the call.

"I have to go. But I'll call Jose tonight. Say hello to everyone back home."

Visibly, by the look on Milo's face and overall body language, he was hung-over. There were dark circles under his eyelids that aged him. He was drained from nights of hooking up with strangers at bars and working in Playa's nightlife district. It's something that he did to keep his DJ skills up to par yet didn't promote fearing more unwanted backlash from his critics. You easily got the impression that Milo was restless and desperate for the pandemic to be over. But just when everybody thought we were leaving Mexico, Milo smiled and dropped a bombshell.

"New Year 's Eve is official, *mis hermanos y hermanas*!" Milo said as everyone listened closely to his rant. "We're going to put on a small, intimate show in a paradise called Bacalar. Some new friends I met in the clubs told me not a lot of tourists know about it yet, so it's fucking perfect! I'm sorry for being distant lately, and I get that some of you want to go home. No stress if you do, by the way. But we can probably agree that our time in Mexico would be a waste if we didn't see other parts of it. I feel like New Year's is the best opportunity for some video content, pics, and all that. It makes the most sense to me. Nobody will be able to talk shit because we can make it clear how deserted and chill Bacalar is! It's a cute little village. And if we do get in trouble or whatever, the go-to excuse can be positive. We can talk about how we want to bring in 2022 with good vibes and endless peace. Mexico has been amazing to us, you know. I never use a mask anymore, and I can see that neither do you guys. So, tell me… what are your thoughts?"

"Great…but what'll happen after the new year?" Sarah asked, an associate editor on Joie Media. The only thing I knew about her was that she always liked Jennifer's LinkedIn posts.

"Well, that's a good question. But honestly, I want to stay in Mexico at least until March or whenever spring break fever comes to light. I want to play shows in Tulum, Puerto Vallarta,

Cancun, and everywhere else. It's obvious things are great. Why do you even want to go home?"

"Some of us need to go home, though," Daniel from the sales team said. "I know I speak for a lot of us, but we can't stay here forever. We need to get back to reality sometime soon, right?"

"Yeah, technically, you can," Milo said after a pause. "But not before the new year, okay? We need everybody here for the music video. Anyway...let's get back to it team! Great work."

When Milo got up and left Chez Celine, it was past noon. I figured that if I wrote my blog articles for the day quickly, I'd be able to call Jose at 5:00 p.m. or something like that. But then, Milo texted me and asked to speak with me in private. Suddenly, my insides froze up with angst.

Around 12:30 p.m., I got back to the hotel and knocked on his room's door—nobody else was in sight other than the cleaning ladies. Milo's place was by far the nicest one. It was a luxury only the richest people could afford. For a minute, the image of Milo's rundown apartment in The Plateau came to mind. I thought of how far he came from those years. But when Milo called me over to sit on one of the couches, my anxiety turned to fear. I tried my best to remain calm.

I remember seeing email notifications on my phone before entering Milo's room—two from job applications and one from a small publisher. It was exciting, yet I tried not to let it show much. Maybe Milo would fire me just for my next chapter to lift me off into my next adventure. I also thought I'd be able to give *la familia* in Mexico better support. But once I sat down with Milo that early afternoon, I felt a troubling dark energy. Milo had bottles of liquor everywhere.

"I got a surprise for you, brother," Milo said, placing himself closer to me with a piece of paper. "My bad if I weirded you out by pulling you aside. I just didn't want people to get jealous. I don't want them to know just how special you are to me. All you need to do is sign, my dude."

For a moment, chills ran down my spine. Self-consciously, it appeared like my intuition was telling me to get as far away from Milo as possible. He glared at me with determination in his eyes. But that just increased my level of anxiety, making me unsure how to react. Strangely, Milo was able to read into my fear. He inched closer until I smelled his alcohol-riddled breath. What did he plan to do with me? There was no way I'd get out of his room without a fight. But then, I looked at the paper Milo had dropped onto my lap. It was a permanent employee contract.

"Yes, it's exactly what you think it is," Milo said, placing his arm around my shoulders, cracking the kind of evil smile that wouldn't take no for a response. "It's for about three years, with room to negotiate for more when the time comes. You'll also get benefits. Isn't that great?"

"What..." I replied, freezing up as his thigh rubbed against mine. "Can I think about it?"

"Oh, fuck off!" Milo placed his free hand on my leg. "Look, you're going to have two weeks of paid vacation per year, five paid sick days, dental, a phone allowance, internet, life insurance, and so much more. Most people don't get that much unless I trust them. But you have done so well, and I want you... I want you bad. Please, just say yes and sign. Let's be together."

While Milo spoke, he resonated with more confidence. He breathed near my face so profusely that I had a good idea what he was drinking. And internally, I heard myself scream for help. This wasn't the Milo I knew in high school. No, it was someone who led with intimidation.

Better yet, it seemed as though the idea of keeping me around turned him on. Every time I tried to adjust myself on the couch, he grabbed onto my thigh a little tighter. He didn't want me to go anywhere until I complied with his "generous" offer. But just when I mentally prepared to fight Milo away, he shifted his body until he was inches away from my ear. He continued to go over the benefits package. I felt suffocated—under his control, trapped like a fly in the spider's web. That's when my heart palpitations started. So much so, I'm surprised Milo didn't notice.

"The thing is...there's a chance someone from my family in Mexico tested posit—"

"But *we're* your family," Milo whispered. "Didn't you know that already?"

"Yeah, but my uncle might have covid and I need to call him after work—"

"Stop, man," Milo said while latching onto my lap. "Kiss me back. C'mon, just do it. I run this show, brother. Let's fuck things out. We'll sign later, as you wish. Just be with me now."

"I can't make any promises until I know he's okay, though," I said, pushing Milo away from my lips. "Sorry, it's not that I don't appreciate this, but I need to get in a better headspace to make the best decision for myself. Hopefully, you get where I'm coming from...I really do."

A pause. Milo gave me a dirty look that made me sweat.

"Well, I'm sorry for employing you while others are depended on the government for cash, and I'm so fucking sorry for offering you a lot more," Milo snapped. "Max, brother... the Shakespeare of my brand. Forget those cousins in Mexico, okay? Covid is the flu. They won't die. In fact, ninety-nine percent of people lived through the disease. So, relax and just enjoy."

"But I-I can't relax until—"

"Kiss me back!" Milo repeated with contempt and intensity in his eyes. It appeared like he wanted to strangle me, which didn't help my heart beat any slower. "Think of it as one of your tasks for the day... Oh, yeah, you know, that's pretty hot. Do me, or you are on probation."

"I still don't know if we should do this, though—"

"Why? Because you don't think your parents or your family would approve of me?" Milo snapped again. "Do they know the shit we've done? Do they know the love we shared, brother? Maybe I should fucking tell them now, right? Everyone knows me for me. But what about you?"

Suddenly, I couldn't feel my heart anymore. The fear Milo instilled was so powerful that I believed my life ended. But the tears streaming down my face reminded me that I was still alive. It was then Milo's attitude toward me changed. Even though he could be spiteful, there were indications within him at that moment which showed me the Milo I knew before the fame.

"Look, I'm sorry. I didn't mean to go that far, brother. I just really want to work with you for many years to come," Milo said, trying to reassure me. "You know what they say, right? Your network is your net worth. And…I want you to stay in my world forever. Do you get that?"

"No, I understand…but you're right. Maybe I should tell my parents? It's just weird—"

"Life is weird, brother. And the more you realize that, the better off you'll be in whatever you do." Milo pulled me closer until our lips touched. "Now…kiss me like it's part of your job."

On that couch, Milo and I made out until we removed our clothes. I remember pretending to be into it when everything inside me wanted to vanish like a ghost. Milo was sold on the fantasy of us being together, yet I didn't feel the same. And once we both finished, disgust overwhelmed me. Whatever magic we had disappeared a long time ago. I needed to move on from the past. But if you saw Milo's face when I got dressed, you would have thought he was lost in a time capsule. He thought our relationship had a new chapter. I saw madness, pride in his eyes, knowing we shared a moment. Milo expected the world, and that reality scared me to death.

"For as long as we're in Mexico, this contract will be ready for you, brother," Milo said with a smile. "All you gotta say is yes, and you'll have it. You'll have everything that you want."

"Can I take the day to process it?" I needed to think. "Half the day is done, anyway—"

"Hey, no, just take a two-hour break or whatever," Milo said. "I need holiday content to start going out by tonight. I'm going to announce this to everyone soon, but my first three singles of the new album will be released on all platforms this Christmas. That'll show the haters! So, you're going to be replying to a lot of comments, writing blogs, and all that. But for now, just chill. I'm sure you're tired from what we did, so yeah. Go to the beach or something, brother."

* * * *

After I left the hotel room, I bought a cheap SIM card at the first Oxxo near Calle 4 and walked until my feet touched the beach's sand next to the ferry station. Since people go to and from Playa Del Carmen in that area quite often, it was packed in the middle of the afternoon. In fact, I remember watching a show put on by a group of Mayans nearby—they danced, played instruments, and sang their hearts out. But although it was passionate and entertaining, it wasn't enough to get me to forget everything with Milo. He was in my head so endlessly that I thought he was stalking me at a distance. I was starting to get paranoid. Better yet, I felt used, disgusted, and confused about Milo's true intentions. He got me to realize that money or a "contract with benefits" wasn't enough to guarantee my happiness. I wanted mutual respect, dignity, and real support. So, when I found a comfortable spot on the beach to sit down, I placed my new SIM card in my phone with the hope new opportunities would present me all those worthwhile things.

Strangely, that placed an interesting idea inside my head: "What better way to realize my dreams than on the beach where I found the inspiration to chase after what I wanted out of life, to write stories of my own, to welcome the adventures waiting for me, encouraging me to leap toward my future success." I thought about everything Diana told me on *Dia de los Muertos*. And I thought of exploring more than just Puerto Rico and Miami. I saw the ocean's everlasting beauty and horizon as symbolism for my Playa Crush. Everything seemed possible. Looking back now, who knew how those delusions gave me solace at the time. But that energy was inspiring. I took a deep breath, made sure nobody was watching, and opened my email inbox.

"Dear Max,

Thank you for your interest in being a content writer for Global United Media. We regret to inform you that we will not be moving forward with your application at this time. We appreciate your interest in Global United Media and wish you good luck on your job search.

Sincerely,
-Global United Media. "

The other job rejection letter was similar in tone. But the most painful let down was this:

"Dear Max,

Thank you so much for your submission to Generation Lit Magazine. We enjoyed your short story "LATE NIGHT DRIVES TO NOWHERE" and felt the emotion in your writing. Your characters, Robert and Ashley, had great chemistry on the page. We can see you have potential.

However, it isn't right for us at this time. It is not at the same level as our other pieces.

Again, keep up the great work. Please, don't be afraid to submit to us in the future.

Sincerely,
The Generation Lit Magazine team."

Even though it was a nice rejection, the sting of not getting published struck me hard. Thoughts of quitting circulated in my mind. After all, the story *Late Night Drives To Nowhere* centered on a date with two people, which happened to be inspired by the night Diana and I shared on the beach. It came from the heart, yet it wasn't enough. "Fuck, is this even worth it?" I quietly ranted to myself. Reflecting on who I was at that moment, I couldn't seem to rationalize what was the point of being a writer, an artist, a poet with a voice, if one had to deal with assholes that had the power to say no to what came reaped from your soul. It didn't make sense.

During that point of frustration, however, I looked straight at the ocean's picturesque image—recognizing it might've symbolized there was a long way to go until I was ready to leave Milo and Joie Media. For as long as Milo wanted to stay in Mexico to ignore the dark realities of COVID-19, I was stranded too. It seemed like I'd be forever lost in my "career", while also balancing out the romantic vision Milo had. I needed to be courageous, to tell Milo we weren't destined to love each other. The problem was that I didn't know how. But right when I could've used a break from my over-thinking, I spotted Diana walking toward my direction with a smile that almost made me forget about my problems and the sun beaming on my skin. She made her way to me as if she was meant to find me lying around that whole time. I still remember how her positive energy lifted my spirits higher, especially when she greeted me with a kiss on the cheek.

"*Hola, buenas!*" Diana said, cheerfully. "Why are you sad? Or maybe you are *cansado*?"

"Yeah... I'm just tired," I replied, as Diana continued to smile. Even with the ocean in front of me and the people on the beach, it was the only thing I saw. Her presence transported me seamlessly into the version of her world. And I cherished every minute of it. *"Cómo te fue hoy?"*

"The day was good," Diana said, reaching for both my hands. "But now, we enjoy and have such fun! I want more photos today, *y necesitas ayudar*. Come assist me, *Maxito. Ven conmigo!*"

"But how can I even help you? I mean, I'm not really an expert or anything."

"*Vamanos!*" Diana said, showing me two ferry tickets to Cozumel set to leave within the hour. "I was going with a friend, but she can't no more. So, then I see you near, and believe it is meant for us! Do, eh, how do you say? ... you think *que hay un Dios* that has nice plans for us?"

"*Problamente que si*, but in this case... it feels more like dumb luck."

"Luck of Gods if you ask me," Diana said with an irresistible spark in her eyes that could have sold you on anything. "But you do nothing here! At least help, *por favor*? Don't have fear."

"I still don't know if I should go, though—"

"Don't be sad and lonely without reasons, Maxito." Diana talked with such passion and reassurance that it was impossible not to pay attention. That's when I began to notice how much she valued my company, heart, and energy at that moment. She cast me under her spell. But what's more, she gave me the opportunity to cast my own on her with just one word: yes. If I said yes to adventures *con ella*, she'd jump along next to me. For the first time in years, I was reminded of love's powerful ways. "I have people you can see in Cozumel, so you're not alone."

"Okay, *si, si, vamanos*," I said after a pause. "You're right. I'm actually bored."

"Let's go and live then," Diana said, as she dragged me toward the ferry station.

Once Diana and I were on the ferry to Cozumel, the ocean's strong current made for a bumpy ride, the salt water had a pungent smell, and I got a little wet from waves that splashed against the ferry boat during the thirty-minute trip. I almost got sick. But yet, the air which blew constantly in my face reminded me that my soul was worth nurturing. It was good for my mental health. Suddenly, it occurred to me how pointless it was to get upset over something as common as a rejection letter. It didn't matter compared to saying yes to Diana, yes to Cozumel, yes to realized dreams. And once we got to Cozumel, it seemed endless possibilities awaited us there.

Despite Cozumel being a short ferry ride away from Playa, the small island was a lot quieter than its *Quintana Roo* counterpart. You didn't hear music blasting from clubs, the noise of a million conversations happening all at once. It was more peaceful than the bustling streets of Playa. No, Cozumel was for scuba diving and lazy beach days at a resort. You noticed it in the crowds of vacationers who occupied Cozumel's downtown square near its famous clock tower. Honestly, there wasn't much noise or excitement anywhere. But if you looked at

Diana, you would've thought she fell in love at first sight. She found nothing but magic in the air—especially as she took photos of *"el Reloj a Centro"*, families on the go, and people at gift shops. She captured beauty in all things most never would. It was fun seeing through her point of view.

After minutes of walking around, however, Diana led us away from Cozumel's touristy spot and closer to the neighborhoods where its local characters lived. She brought me to the heart of the island. That's when Diana introduced me to her friend Elvio's hostel, where I met a group of people she hung out with on the days she'd be nowhere to be found in Playa Del Carmen. We laughed and drank with her two Canadian scuba instructor friends, a digital nomad from New York, three digital nomads from France, two from Germany, a couple from Argentina, people from other regions of Mexico who moved to Cozumel years ago, and three adopted street dogs.

The group welcomed me into their circle like I was now part of their family dynamic, and we spent time on Elvio's rooftop watching the sunset. It was a friendly environment as we talked about life in Mexico, in Playa Del Carmen, surrounded in paradise, away from the struggles of a pandemic-fuelled world. Suddenly, I couldn't remember why a handful of emails got me down. It felt utterly meaningless. And that's when I recognized Diana showed me how to let go, to appreciate moments that made life worth living. I knew then why her smile was hard to forget.

When Elvio brought everyone tacos from the hostel's restaurant bar, we ate dinner and continued to talk and laugh like we'd all been friends for twenty years. I remember not wanting to leave. But once Diana and I needed to catch the last ferry to Playa, everyone said their goodbyes and invited me to return whenever possible. It was the happiest I've been since the day I heard Bellita yell out "Maxito" at Casa Velasco. That's when thoughts about *mi familia* resurfaced. It inspired me to send a text to Jose, wishing him the best as I strolled with Diana.

Reflecting on this now, we moved as though the universe was at our fingertips—there was no rush to go or be anywhere except the roads of Cozumel, a place where the Mayans ruled with traditions that still carried over to 2021. The moonlight became more evident once we made it to the clock tower, elevating Cozumel's presence from earlier that afternoon. I don't know what Diana was thinking exactly when we got to *el Reloj a Centro*, smelling the salt water as the ferry's last boarding call approached. But as Diana caught a glimpse of how the moonlight shined down on us, she quickly stopped to take her photos. Nobody loved art more than she did.

Honestly, who knew what caught her attention in particular: the moon or how Cozumel's *Reloj a Centro* looked beneath it. The source of her inspiration could've also come from the downtown square's charm, which became more apparent since most people were now back at their resorts. But Diana had a talent for showing you her emotions when it came to her passions, the part of her which couldn't turn down a moment to be creative. She went with the flow, exploring all that intrigued her. But yet, Diana was the "flow". It's what made her so original.

"Say to me *que tu piensas?*" Diana asked, observing me with eyes that were filled with color. "What is for you a good photo? I'm curious enough with you. What is your great vision?"

"I don't know, really? Maybe… friends playing beach volleyball or something?"

"No, no, no, never like this," Diana said with amusement. "You can find those images *facilmente en la playa* and it is of no interest. Tell me, what speaks personally to you? Be authentic, don't go with what others think. That's the difference between good photos and bad."

"What's funny is, I used to believe I was a talented, creative person with an eye for good content," I said, while Diana continued to head toward the ferry station at a calm pace. "But compared to you… I'm nothing. I don't think I'm close. Please, teach me. I could use your help."

I recognize the last part was exaggerated. But I was in a strange mood, thinking about Casa Velasco, my new friends in

Cozumel, and especially the career I was returning to in Playa. The idea of living on a small island forever suddenly became appealing. Looking back, maybe Diana heard my internal monologue. She wanted me to experience that lifestyle. She was kind enough to embrace the challenge of opening up my horizons. Better yet, she showed me compassion.

"Oh, with pleasure I teach you everything!" Diana said as we reached the ferry station fifteen minutes before the last boarding call. "Go and walk by these white benches over here."

Until we had to get on the ferry, Diana kept taking photos while I stood before the white-tiled benches that outlined Cozumel's dock and where late-night strolls appeared magical. Cozumel's simple charm found a place in my heart. It was great to engage in Diana's process, being introduced to a slice of her universe. The more direction she gave me, the more she told me how to position myself like an "Instagram influencer". And despite the fact there are many pages in my notebook to describe that night, I can never depict those hours with enough justice.

"*Qué guapo, qué guapo!*" Diana said, showing me the photos once we were halfway to Playa. "See how you are? The way you seem in touch with surroundings? You can't replicate it."

"Definitely better than I would've ever guessed," I said, a little surprised at how good the photos turned out. We soaked up each other's company until the ferry dropped us off on Playa's tourist strip. Photos continued to be taken as we stopped at a great *pizzeria* near Calle 6. It was an experience with Diana that felt glorious and filled with the most positive energy you could find. Time was non-existent. But then my phone vibrated. It was Milo, asking where I had gone.

"You need to work again?" Diana asked, staring at me like she didn't want me to leave.

"I don't want to, but have no choice," I said with reluctance. "It sucks, but whatever."

"I hope you have a life someday with no whatevers," Diana said, as though she expected a response like that. "But for now…I'm glad that you're here. *Me gusta cuando estamos juntos.*"

"Me too. Hey, so… should I just travel to Cozumel next time I can't find you in Playa?" I said, after a pause. "I know you like to disappear. Even when I text you, there isn't a response."

She laughed.

"Tengo amigos en todas partes de Mexico," Diana said, flirtatiously hitting my arm. "I get my work done some days, and others I take with me *por inspiracion* and to relax. I need balance en la vida, *entiendes?* We all need it. Maybe next time you meet more *amigos.* They're so cool."

* * * *

Roughly at 10:30 p.m., I got back to my hotel room, took a shower, and got ready to put out a blog article centered on Milo's hits from the new album going into Bacalar that December, and a newsletter email designed to excite his followers more about what was planned for the new year. Suddenly, the realities of work came back into full swing as I made up for the hours I missed that day, leading me to feel trapped, frustrated, sick and tired of working for Milo's brand. But once Diana posted the beautiful content she took in Cozumel, Milo texted me aggressively to question what I did on my "two-hour break". The argument went on until 3:00 a.m. But the photos generated a lot of likes by that time, which looked good for Milo since his fans knew we were part of Joie Media. That's what eventually got him to calm down, along with me promising him I'd "never do something like that again." It was a relief when he finally left me alone, yet the micromanaging was terrifying. Milo behaved like a jealous, insecure boyfriend.

During that time, I kept thinking about Bellita, Jose, *mis primos*, and everyone else back in Mexico City and Casa Velasco. It helped distract me from Milo's bullshit that night, yet at the same time, made me grow more with concern. Honestly, I didn't understand why I couldn't get Bellita out of my mind in particular. Was the universe telling me something?

Was it God? It was hard to know for sure. But when I tried to call *mi familia* the next morning, nobody answered.

PART 3:

THE PAIN & THE BEAUTY

Chapter 13

December 31, 2021

Bacalar was filled with a peaceful aura that even the greatest poet wouldn't be able to put into words. It was nothing like other parts of Mexico I had visited so far. And for the life of me, I didn't understand why it was still a relatively unknown destination in *Quintana Roo*—at least among people not from Mexico, or those who haven't spent enough time in the country to be tipped off about that beautiful gem like Milo was back in Playa. Bacalar was *un pueblo* surrounded by lagoons, *cenotes*, a Mayan ruin preserved for visitors to check out free of charge, boats, and dirt roads. These were places I discovered my first two mornings. Every time you jumped into the water to go on the swings they had laid out on each boardwalk, your skin felt smoother once you got out. Every time I walked around the small village, a new street dog greeted me out of nowhere, a delicious *taqueria* presented itself, and quiet little neighborhoods with people who smiled at you when you made eye contact came to light. I was in God's version of paradise. But near the Mayan ruins, you also noticed construction sites— meant to welcome more people in future years, to accommodate and entertain tourists to help their economy grow.

Granted, there were people from Europe, Canada, and Latin America I met in Bacalar, yet it was nothing compared to the number of tourists in Playa or Tulum. In fact, mostly everyone I talked to by the lagoons were digital nomads who had spent months living in Mexico before even knowing about Bacalar's existence. It almost seemed like Mexico's best-kept secret, the type of location that wasn't heavily advertised online. It wasn't populated by too many visitors or locals. It wasn't overcome with technology and social media. It didn't lose its original essence. And it seemed I got to Bacalar at the right time—just before it became a popular tourist destination. Even now, I still dream of Bacalar's moonlight. It was the perfect spot to fall in love.

Everyone at Joie Media was excited about the New Year's event, especially since it fell under our week off for the holidays from December 27 to January 3 of 2022. The only thing Milo wanted from us was footage of him DJing for content creation purposes. Bacalar had one bar with an open dance floor walking distance from the Mayan ruins, which lit up brightly in the evening. The stars and the moon decorated the sky with ease. Excitement was in the air. It's where we planned to welcome the new year. It's where Milo wanted to have his last show of 2021. But despite our plans, there was a sense of guilt about how blessed I was at that moment.

Back in Montreal, the new Omicron variant made the Quebec government enforce a curfew and stricter lockdown, killing all New Year's plans that were organized in the province. It got me to think about my family and friends, hoping they'd be okay. I thought about *mi familia*, wondering if they were playing it safe this New Year's, staying out of reach from being infected. But with the slow Wi-Fi Bacalar had, I decided to keep off my phone before worrying too much.

Roughly around 8:00 p.m., we made our way to the New Year's event at an outdoor terrace called *"I Scream Bar"*, where every two minutes the bar owner gave his employees the queue to scream out to the Mayan gods who overlooked Bacalar. It was an environment that reflected everything Milo loved about the clubs in Playa, a lively enthusiasm for good times that didn't slow down for anyone. It exhibited the kind of vibe Milo fed into with his DJ sets, which made the locals of Bacalar overwhelmed with excitement since it wasn't every day a celebrity wanted to play a show in their small village as opposed to a party destination like Cancun or Tulum. It was a big deal, and the attention of their phones recording every second of

Milo's appearance fed more into his ego. I remember the crowd growing bigger as the New Year's event progressed. Word of mouth spread of Milo's presence. And by 10:00 p.m., the bar was packed.

Milo's vision, in retrospect, for an intimate New Year's party changed. Nobody expected to have a crowd like the one we had. But yet, Milo embraced it all, wanting nothing more than to welcome 2022 in with a bang, a statement, and a feeling that couldn't be replicated anywhere else. His playlist was designed to go all night long if he needed it to, and trust me, it seemed Milo was on a mission to shift Bacalar's peaceful aura into a rhythmic one that would inspire endless dance parties. Everyone who showed up to I Scream Bar knew Milo was going to play his latest singles, remixes of popular songs, old favorites, and other surprises in between. When some of the videos of Milo's performance circulated online, they went viral in milliseconds. Suddenly, hundreds of people who commented on Instagram wished to be in Bacalar that night.

Looking back on things now, we were in one of the remaining parts of the world that was untouched by the pandemic. Everyone in Bacalar was free to relish their evenings —drunken souls who were fortunate enough to celebrate life, to maintain their hope for better days to come during what was a strange time for everyone. Fears of getting sick were kicked to the side. Honestly, I forgot the pandemic existed in given moments. But the more I drank, the harder it was to stop thinking of my loved ones. The last thing I wanted was to be with Milo and my team.

Since the last journal entry, my routine became somewhat predictable: I'd fill out job applications and submit queries to publishers in the morning, I'd work until around 6:00 p.m., eat dinner, meet with Milo at our Playa hotel lobby, sometimes hook up, shower, and then hang out with Diana the rest of the night. It was a vicious cycle, yet one that was also normal. The more I slept with Milo, the more he'd add to my permanent employment contract. The more his old feelings became reignited. But the problem was, he wasn't the one my heart desired to have most. I didn't have the courage to tell him the truth. After all, by the New Year's event, things got quite messy and complicated. I ended up signing a five-year contract to work for Joie Media that included good benefits, health insurance, a phone allowance, an internet allowance, three weeks of paid vacation, a week of paid sick days, and a "guarantee" of career advancement. I'd be lying to myself if I didn't sign up for job security reasons. But secretly, I also did it to remain close to Diana. If I quit working for Milo, I feared losing her just as our relationship blossomed.

The minute I signed the contract, though, Milo became more affectionate, yet controlling. He texted me several times a day, called me "just to talk" at random points of the night, and always wanted to "come over". I hated myself for settling and thinking I wasn't good enough to be hired somewhere else. It didn't seem like I had the chops to be a published author, either. Something was wrong, yet I couldn't figure it out. Even during the New Year's Eve party, I turned on my limited phone data to check my inbox. I kept hoping for a chance to build my next chapter and a newfound belief in my self-worth. But this was the only type of email I received in December. It was the same old story with the same bullshit result. It made me want to scream.

"Dear Max,

Thank you so much for your interest in the role of Staff Writer for Newsweek Toronto Media. However, we're sorry to say we will not move forward with your application.

We greatly appreciate your interest in Newsweek Toronto Media and hope you will continue to look for other job opportunities on our website."

After a while, the act of job hunting became draining. It led me to sign a contract I wasn't a hundred percent invested in out of desperation. Unemployment wasn't a viable option by any means—especially on the road in Mexico. Life didn't seem fair at that time, and the melancholy of seeing others brag about their career successes on LinkedIn wasn't good for my mental health.

Maybe I wasn't that great of a writer? But despite the negativity coursing through me, two things helped me stay motivated. Most of the authors who were part of the Lost Generation in 1920s' Paris developed classic novels from pain. It came after a brutal war. It came after the Spanish Flu pandemic. Art was conceived. New ways of modernism and life shone in the forefront of people's minds. And in the darkness came great works. If you saw the crowd at the bar as I did, you got the feeling a new lost generation was emerging. It inspired me to keep on writing, to document my future "lost generation experiences". Maybe 2022 would be the perfect time for me to write a novel? And if that happened, I wanted Diana to become immortalized.

Amazingly, Diana knew everyone that worked at I Scream Bar from the bartenders, the security, the people who incited "screaming" and dancing, and even the regular street dogs who occasionally wandered in and out. She knew the residents of Bacalar who came out that evening. And she greeted many different groups, including these nice Dutch people at our hotel and a pair of couples she claimed to have met in Puerto Escondito. She was everywhere at once. It was clear Diana was embraced in various Mexican communities. That's when I ordered more drinks at the bar. Jealous thoughts were emerging inside me and I didn't know how else to control them. But strangely, the harder it was to keep her in my life, the more I wanted to love Diana forever.

That night, it didn't take long to see Diana loved to socialize, to make new connections, to be everyone's best friend. She was the heart of Bacalar, the light which guided people's fire to have a good time. Looking back, I should've thought about what Hugo, Sara, and Manuel said about her at Casa Velasco. Maybe, then, I wouldn't have been so anxious to have Diana for myself to share a memorable New Year's kiss at midnight. It's hard to say why I felt that way. But one thing is for sure: I should've prioritized calling *mi familia* a little better.

My focus should have been on the ones who cared about me the most, rather than checking my phone for updates on jobs that I'd never get. All I knew was Jose might've had Omicron. Even with two vaccines, he got infected—making me scared for Bellita. I wished to God when I called them to say *"Feliz Ano Nuevo!"*, they'd all be in good health. It's something I hoped to tell my parents too.

When 10:30 p.m. hit, Milo got his video team to call me to the main stage. He wanted to get footage of us together. Milo had grabbed my hand and raised it to the crowd. I remember how we vibed to the songs he played. The adrenaline was unreal, and pictures taken of our moment would most likely get attention online. We danced, we fed into each other's rhythm, and Milo even kissed me on the cheek several times. But at one point, Diana was capturing footage and taking pics, giving me a thumbs up as we made eye contact. The moment I let out a smile, she reciprocated. I read her lips and noticed she was trying to give me direction like our night in Cozumel. It was a funny exchange between us that nobody else seemed to recognize. We spoke our own language within our own universe. Suddenly, the night was filled with more possibility and excitement. Eventually, though, Diana ventured off to another part of the bar for content purposes. And that's when I remember telling Milo I had to use the bathroom for a second.

"Are you kidding me, brother?" Milo said, annoyed. "Look at the crowd. And look at the fucking time… We only got an hour! Hold it in, okay? I'm not letting you go. You can't now."

"No worries, I'll be back in time for the countdown—"

"Shut up, asshole!" Milo snapped with rage in his eyes. He hated being distracted from his DJ sets. Shamelessly, I used it to my advantage. "Fine, alright…just make it quick. We need an epic shot of us welcoming in 2022 together. It's for our content, brother, so it's really important."

Finding myself near the bar area minutes later, I was practicing my Spanish with Diana and her Bacalar friends. It wasn't memorable, yet I recalled one interesting thing when someone mentioned the construction sites near the Mayan ruins.

"Soon we have *parques* and other stuff *para las turistas*," Heraldo said, a boat operator and diving instructor from Monterrey. "Five years before, Tulum was nothing. Just lagoons. But today, everyone goes. We hope the same happens with Bacalar." The way Heraldo spoke carried endless optimism. And in my drunken state, it made me reflect on how quickly beautiful things could be ruined with mainstream attention, social media influencers, overrated tourist attractions, pricey restaurants, and resorts that killed a place's unique charm. It made me wonder if Bacalar's peaceful aura would disappear if it someday got popular. I prayed to the Mayan gods above it would never happen.

Distracting me from that scary idea, however, was a storm of people that wanted to reach the bar for a drink before midnight. It was just past 11:00 p.m., and the party was raging. So much so, it appeared impossible to push through the crowd surrounding Milo. But I realized I'd be in trouble if I didn't at least try to make it back. Diana somehow found herself on the opposite side of the bar with other people, anyway, and it occurred to me I'd never have a private moment with her before midnight. That's when I headed toward Milo's little stage, waving at him while I moved. He didn't see me once. But then, something happened. I met a group of digital nomads.

"Hey, aren't you that Canadian I met in Tulum two months ago?" this drunken guy said, excitedly tapping my shoulder. "Yeah, it was in Straw Hat's bar upstairs! I think it's you, though, at least... because he told me he'd be traveling around Mexico like us. But I forget his name."

He was in a group of five. All of them seemed happy to see me, whoever they thought I was. But I welcomed in their energy. Meeting new friends on the road is one of the best parts of it.

"No, I haven't actually gone to Tulum yet, believe it or not!" I replied. "But I do happen to be Canadian, though, so you got something about me right. Anyway, so where are you from?"

"You need to before you leave Mexico," a woman in the group said with a smile. "The blue waters, the parties, the biking, the Mayan ruins, it's all incredible. Go when you leave Bacalar!"

After a little more conversation, we followed each other on Instagram and shared a few laughs. The drunken guy's name was Ramon, a Canadian from Toronto who worked as a digital marketer. The woman was another Canadian named Alexia, a social media manager at a real estate company just outside of Vancouver. The other three people were a Quebecois named Matt, and two people from Chile and Mexico City named Eddie and Stefania. They all met in the last three months and forged a strong bond. Every day, they planned adventures with each other —making TikTok videos of their experiences, writing travel blog content, and engaging with their digital nomad community. Bizarrely, I got the feeling we met for a reason. They were inspiring.

"I don't exactly know when we'll leave Mexico, dude, because we all know how crazy our government is acting right now," Ramon said, at one point. "We might take a detour in Belize and then come straight back here. It's wild...but I hope things calm down sometime this year."

"Same here!" Matt said. "I want to teach scuba diving in Cancun to stay even longer."

"Look around you. Honestly. I feel like everyone tonight is getting away from something pandemic-related," Alexia said, while everyone nodded. "It's not humanly natural to be isolated from people for two years and it shows. Imagine all the mental health problems going on, right?"

"Screw the pandemic! It's gotten way out of hand," Ramon said, rolling his eyes.

"It's a cold," Matt said. "Nothing more. The media just likes to exaggerate it."

"Yeah, for real," Alexia said. "Most people will survive even if they do get sick."

"I got it and I recovered well," Eddie said. "Don't believe everything the media say."

"True," Alexia said. "At the end of the day, they're just trying to draw some traffic."

"If it bleeds, it fucking leads, unfortunately," Ramon said. "Don't buy into that crap."

"But I'm thankful this is not us!" Stefania said. "Let's get drinks and pray for next year."

"*Orale!*" Eddie said. "The pandemic is shit in Mexico, too, *pero* we still need to live."

Feeling engaged in the group dynamic, we cheered for the new year to come with tequila shots. But at the same time, I was on the lookout for Diana and other people from Joie Media. Connecting to the data on my phone, I decided to text Milo that I was "on my way" back to the stage where he played. I also messaged Diana to ask if she was at the bar. Looking back now, everyone was probably close to Milo. But that night, I saw my life going in a direction that I wanted to embrace. My new friends had justified remarks about the pandemic, yet their criticism just made me think about *mi familia* more heavily. Had Jose spread COVID-19 to others? Was Clarisa taking care of him since she was a nurse? What did 2022 have in store? Would it be the year the pandemic finally ends? That's when I messaged everyone—Hugo, Sara, Manuel, Jose, Clarisa, and Bellita. I also sent my parents, sister, and friends in Montreal messages online—all of which were at home, complaining about the government canceling major New Year's events.

But right before my mind continued to go into a dark place, Milo announced that we were "ten seconds away from 2022". He began to count down in Spanish, as my new group handed me another tequila shot. And once 2021 was over, Milo blasted to the crowd a new remix of "Joie de Vivre" to ignite the crowd with nostalgia and delight. Spirits were now at their highest.

Everyone danced their hearts out, hugging and kissing each other like the pandemic was a thing of the past. Life was restored—euphoria, optimism, and positive vibes soared high in the Bacalar evening air. We were all free in that little-known, beautiful, intimate *pueblo* in Quintana Roo. But although I was enjoying the party, I couldn't help but suddenly feel alone.

Anxiety about my immediate future kicked in. Would all my job-hunting lead to something? Would 2022 be good for me? Before I started to cry, I excused myself from my new group for a moment.

Leaving the bar altogether, I walked until I got to a restaurant's terrace area neighboring the venue. It was close enough that I was able to still hear Milo's DJ set but far enough to be able to hide from people for a while. There were no streetlights near the restaurant, which made me feel alone in my own darkness. Nobody answered when I called *mi familia*, despite trying at least a hundred times. Maybe, if I went back to my hotel, I'd have a better Wi-Fi connection. The lack of being able to hear Jose or Bellita's voice drove me further into despair. But when I decided to head back to the party to say my goodbyes before calling it a night, Diana headed toward me with a *marquesita*—a street food, *un dulce* you could find anywhere in Mexico. I'll never forget the expression on Diana's face once we made eye contact. She gladly came to join me on that terrace, as if to reassure me that we'd get through the darkness together. In my drunken state, it felt like genuine love. My heart raced so quickly it was a little bit painful. The night wasn't over.

"Where do you go this entire time?" Diana asked, showing me her phone. "Look, *mira*, I was going to write you. We searched in all parts, *entiendes*? Milo ask us, and now I find you here in the last place I expect to see you near. Why do you go away, Max? Are you happy tonight?"

"Sorry... I mean, yeah," I replied, looking at my phone to see the texts I didn't know I had before. "I was looking for you, too. But I met new friends *y después*... I needed to be alone."

"Isn't it nice to meet new encounters?" Diana said as she gave me her *marquesita*. "Have you tried these before? I like them immensely. I eat it *con* nutella *y plátanos. Tienen buen gusto.*"

"Not really, but now I consider this my favorite new encounter tonight," I said, making Diana laugh. I had a bite of the *marquesita* and smiled to express my approval of her good taste.

"I'll say to everyone and Milo you cannot be found *conmigo*," Diana said, messaging our team and putting her phone away without even a second thought. "You're funnier and nicer to be with, *yo creo*. I like you alone. I like how we are peaceful here. It's my Bacalar and my Mexico."

"Damn, how did you become so cool?" I said, giving her back the *marquesita*. "Honestly, though, what's your secret? I feel like I can apply it to my own life somehow. Or I'll at least try."

"I'm not cool, *que dices*?" Diana said, before slowly reaching for my ear. "But I do not care what all people believe. You should not either. Be free from what keeping you from enjoying."

"I missed you at midnight," I said, as Diana approached closer to me with no intention of leaving my side. She reached out for my hand, hypnotizing me with her presence. "And in case I haven't told you, *creo que tu eres bonita como las estrellas*. You're perfect just how you are."

All of a sudden, Diana turned quiet. But I saw her eyes rage with a million thoughts in her head. She blushed, she twirled her hair, and she didn't want this moment of ours to end. It seemed like Diana appreciated my honest words. Looking back, there was a chance for us that night. But more importantly, we had a fresh start in 2022 to figure everything out. There was something romantic and beautiful about it. And I got the feeling Diana knew it too—there was no way she didn't in our special, burning moment. Right then, I thought of my Mayan horoscope. Maybe, Diana was the "one person" I'd love forever. It was something I hoped would manifest.

"Want to go walking?" Diana said, taking my hand. "Come, let's go see *las estrellas*."

Before long, we strolled along Bacalar until we got past the Mayan ruins, toward an even quieter area than the one around the restaurant. The noise of Milo's DJ set became less and less evident the further we had gone. But yet, it was a mistake to do that because of one reason: the unpredictable nature of tropical weather. Funny enough, the rain in Quintana Roo usually came when you least expected it to happen. And when the next surprise rainstorm came along that night, Diana and I found shelter under a rooftop covering a little market's fruit stand. I continued to hold Diana's hand, yet wasn't sure if it was appropriate to make a move. Something about my nerves drew Diana closer. Her heart pressed against mine. It appeared to me she wanted to feel my emotions. She read into my body language. But mostly, her body was guiding mine to think the way hers did. She possessed a sexy-cute energy that was irresistible. From the outside, our stroll was uneventful. But it was a magical instance that seemed written a long time ago by the Mayans. It felt powerful to believe we were meant to love. Thanks to the Mayans, this was fate.

"Cómo te sientes ahora?" Diana asked, breaking the silence. "I want to know, *amigo.*"

"Good... actually, it's hard to explain," I said. "I'm just worried about *mi familia*. Jose, *mi tio*, got covid. And now, I'm scared *mis primos* will be infected. I can't get it out of my head."

"Sometimes, I have many worries *para mi familia tambien,*" Diana said. "But the covid is not so major, *entiendes*? You get it and then it goes. I wish nobody to be sick, but probably not."

"Maybe you're right?" I said, after a pause. "I don't know anyone who died from covid."

Suddenly, Diana placed her hands on my cheeks.

"That's so beautiful, however," Diana said. "To care is a wonderful quality in people."

"Yeah, I guess so? I actually want to go to Mexico City to check up on *mi tio y primos*. I don't know why... but I just feel I need to do that. It's like the universe is telling me something."

"See above more," Diana said, pointing with excitement. "Your answers lie in the sky. It's what *los Mayas* did for guidances years before. What you say is coming from this, so keep exploring your instincts. Remember, Maxito, honesty is art. If it not so original from you, it'll never be clear. No regrets *en la vida*, you know what I say? Your words are clear, so *dime mas.*"

The rain kept coming down hard, yet it wasn't noticeable anymore. We teleported into our version of a romance novel. Feeling Diana's warmth, I knew this had to be the part where our characters became one, to feel something beyond who we were, to have a place somewhere in the galaxy to reveal our mutual affection. All I had to do was tell Diana my heart ached only for her. There was something about Diana's light that encouraged me to keep her in my arms, to give in to our breathtaking moment, to run away forever, and never look back. I wanted her to come with me to Mexico City if she'd join me on that adventure. Purpose seemed to direct me the longer I stared into Diana's eyes and realized she wanted all the things I did too. I needed to take a shot now before the real world resurfaced to disrupt it. Or, before Milo called my phone.

"I don't want to regret anything. It's just that I think you're really beautiful, special, and creative," I said. "I like you. I want you. And I'll do whatever I can not to lose this connection. My life is never going to be the same now that I've met you. It won't and I'm happy to know—"

"Then make the connection!" Diana said, gently pulling my shirt until our lips touched.

Naturally, I froze on the inside as we kissed. But the more I let go, the more I realized how deeply and intensely my emotions were for my *Playa Crush*. Reflecting on that New Year's, Diana's heart wanted my love just as much. It was all meant to happen somehow in the Bacalar rain, isolated from every living soul around, deserted without a Wi-Fi connection. I gave in to the energy that surfaced, an unspoken current of passion and bliss with each second we kissed. The closer Diana got to me in that little market, the more my love for her grew. It was just past 1:00 a.m., and for most, the party was about to wind down. But to us, the night was going in slow motion. I didn't know if I was dead tired or under Diana's spell—sold on the fantasy that we created together. Strangely, the future made me smile. Hope returned and the feeling was indescribable. Reflecting on all this, it was the last time I recall ever being like that.

"I want Mexico City *contigo*," Diana said, out of nowhere. "Go and I'll follow you after."

"Wait, but… are you sure?" I replied, caught off guard. "I don't even know if I can yet."

"Yes, you will," Diana said, reaching for my ear. *"Puedo oír las estrellas como tú."*

Chapter 14

January 9, 2022

Suddenly, I began to gain momentum in my quest for a new job. Over the last week, I did a handful of first-round interviews, emailed blog samples to well-known media outlets, and even made professional connections on LinkedIn. Every interview I had made me feel better about my chances. Every time I made talent acquisition specialists laugh or smile, the more confident I became. Reflecting on things now, however, none of them ever cared I was in their "network" hoping for the kind of exciting news they had the power to give people. Most of the recruiters I came across never contacted me again. It seemed integrity and kindness didn't exist anymore.

But I got so occupied with all the online chats I had with Bellita that I didn't have time to recognize the neglect I was experiencing in the corporate world. When she read the "Happy New Year" message I sent her in Bacalar, communicating with Bellita became a normal part of my daily routine. She told me about the salsa classes she attended, the people she encountered in her neighborhood with Abuela Velasco, and how she liked seeing her friends. Earlier this January, Bellita even surprised me with a video call that included everyone at Casa Velasco in it and that made me feel loved. Better yet, I forgot about the companies that were ghosting me so blatantly. I began to feel good about my self-worth, knowing it was enough for *todo mi familia* in Mexico.

Despite all their love, though, I decided to keep the best news I got that year to myself. I received positive feedback from a mid-sized literary magazine about the short story I wrote after the New Year's I spent with Diana. Maybe I feared telling people because of what they'd all think. But after many other rejections, "Songs of the Mayans" appeared to be my breakthrough.

The story *Songs of the Mayans* followed a young Falcon-born man named Carlos that comes across a mystic in Chichen Itza. Later, he sees the "love of his life" in a dream, becomes obsessed with the idea of being "hers", and goes out in search of the mystery girl on a wild night in Playa. I wanted to keep the memories of what happened in Bacalar to myself, almost like a secret for Diana and me to remember. It was so intimate and perfect that I couldn't ruin it if, by chance, the story got published. I'd never forgive myself if I damaged the sentiment of our night.

I submitted the first half to the magazine two days after the New Year's party without expecting a response. It wasn't my best work since I didn't leave room for my imagination to fictionalize things better. It was mostly all true. But I'm glad of that chance in retrospect—listening to my gut and intuition. I remember almost crying when *The Montreal Arts* requested the full manuscript. My mood soared during the first week of 2022. It was a sense of happiness that reflected glowingly when I'd see Milo, talk to coworkers, and especially when I hung out with Diana. But on that Sunday morning, a video call from my parents changed my life forever.

"Did you hear about Bellita's grandmother?" my mother said, trying to hold back tears. "She just tested positive for covid. We think she got it from your uncle or someone at his *taqueria*. I'm sure you know about the New Year's party they had... God, I hope she'll be okay."

For a minute or two, I hesitated on the phone, unsure how to react. An overwhelming sense of guilt hit me to the point where I almost fainted. Knowing my mother, she'd never accept the truth. Even though Bellita regularly texted me, we never had in-depth conversations. I was as clueless as my parents were in Montreal. After Bacalar, Milo's schedule was a hectic one. I wouldn't have spoken to anyone outside of my coworkers if it wasn't for Bellita. But yet, there was nothing I could've done to slow down Milo's lifestyle. He played shows in Tulum and Playa before ending up at the Oasis Hotel in Cancun—a resort made for partying and younger crowds.

Cancun, to me and everyone else, was a hotspot for American families on vacation, some Canadians, and people on their way to *Isla Mujeres*. You noticed it in the huge buffets that were laid out in resorts. You saw it on the beaches. From a marketing perspective, you could see Cancun had a defined audience they wanted to please. But Milo loved the Oasis since they were treating him like royalty, hoping he'd sign on to a residency at their hotel for spring break in March. It fueled his ego. And as a result, Milo's busy schedule made everyone on the team even busier. I wrote social media posts, newsletters, and a blog series Milo called his *"Luxurious Cancun World"*. Ninety percent of my time was dedicated to work, as I used the rest for job hunting. But I couldn't say it like that to my mom. So, I put on a "show" of my own pretending to be informed about everything. I'm not proud in retrospect, yet I felt like I didn't have a choice.

"Wait, are you sure?" I said after a pause. "I mean, how do you know it was from the *taqueria*? I know they had a New Year's party... but I don't remember how many people came."

"She might've also gotten it at the market near her apartment building," my mother said. "Or maybe it was a combination of a lot of different things. I know you're working hard with Milo, but I thought you most likely heard something from your cousins. Did you talk to them?"

"No, you're right... I saw a post online that they all gathered at the *taqueria* for the party. But my cousins have jobs, too, so it's hard to talk every minute. It's not possible, unfortunately. I mean, now I'm in Cancun, and two days earlier I was in Tulum. Travel also makes it a struggle."

"Fair enough, but—" My mother cut off. "Anyway, your father wants to talk to you."

I waited as my mother gave him the phone.

"Hey, how's it going?" my father said, breaking the ice. "Are you enjoying Mexico?"

"Thankfully, we don't have Montreal weather here, so it's been pretty good."

"Yes, but the peak season is now over," he said. "Maybe you don't know this, but after the first week of January, it gets much colder in Mexico. And sometimes in Quintana Roo, where you are in Cancun, it rains for many days. How much longer are you staying? We all miss you."

"I can't really say because Milo is waiting on the video team to edit content that was shot on New Year's, and now a potential long-term residency in Cancun might happen. Maybe we—"

"At least go to Mexico City for a little bit," my father said with quiet desperation in his voice. "We know you work from your laptop, and you deserve a break. It's for family, it's for Bellita, and it's for your own good. We all need to be together. And since we all can't, it's up to you to represent us. Pray with them. Bring positive spirits. Tell Milo today. He'll understand."

During the pause that followed, the words "it's for Bellita" stuck out in a way I didn't expect. I thought of the little effort I put in to connect with her. She told me so much about her daily life, yet I only talked about work. She never really knew me, and it's painful for me to recognize. But when my father gave the phone to my mother, the universe emphasized that point.

"One more thing," she said. Her eyes were filled with concern. "Please, please, tell us if Bellita needs anything from us. Her *abuela* is her best friend and has been like a second mother to her for years. She loves you... so maybe take her out to eat or do something to cheer her up."

"Actually, the funny thing is I did just sign a new contract that states I'm entitled to seven paid days off," I said, realizing I didn't tell my parents the good news yet. It was a strange type of feeling because it should've been a given on my part. It appeared my work-life balance was more irrelevant than I thought. "So, I'll just book time off in the system we have, and then get set to be in Mexico City tomorrow if it's possible. I'll go check out some flight deals later tonight."

"*Felicidades,* Maxito!" my father said with a smile, replacing the concerned looks from before. "Sounds like a promotion. And I'm so proud you have a career you enjoy. Tell everyone we'll come to Mexico soon so that we can all be together. Please… say that we hope Abuela Velasco will recover quickly. Tell them we missed them and that we will be praying in Canada."

After our conversation ended, guilt continued to ache my heart. That's when it became clear I needed another job. It was time to be brave enough to leave Joie Media—for Bellita, *mi familia*, my parents, and my own peace of mind. And with my new contract and the promising opportunities I had received lately, perhaps it was for the best to go my own way after Cancun.

Clicking around on a discount travel site, I found a flight to Mexico City departing tomorrow night. I booked my ticket, requested a day off in Joie Media's system, and called *mis primos* to let them know I was coming. Everyone was happy, and a part of me felt whole again. Manuel also mentioned he'd tell Bellita once she got to the *tacquiera* for her shift, which made me feel happier. But there was one thing I had to do before anything happened: I needed to tell Milo as a courtesy. And since we hooked up a bunch of times in 2022, it wouldn't be difficult.

Even as I reflect, I'll never forget my nerves once I texted Milo to "meet". In fact, my anxiety got worse as I got to his room. But it was official—I bought a non-refundable ticket. Milo opened the door and kissed me on the lips. He thought we'd just have another regular sexual encounter when I arrived. But self-consciously, I knew we couldn't be anymore. With the ticket info on my phone giving me confidence, I was ready to go. It was the beginning of the end.

"Look at you coming through at the right time, brother!" Milo said with a laugh. "I've been stressed lately, so I'm not down to talk much. But we can let our bodies do the talking, am

I right? Let's just explore like we've been doing. Tell me what your needs are, and they'll be met."

Milo took off his clothes, hypnotizing me for a second. I lost all sense of reality and found myself drawn to the nostalgia of past dreams. I remembered the way I admired Milo back in his old apartment. The energy had been weird ever since I ditched him to be with Diana in Bacalar. And maybe, I was trying to recapture something between us that was lost. Is this why I drew so heavily from that old memory, all of a sudden? It's something I had in mind as I started to undress. But in my confusion, I got a message that gave me perspective when I needed it most.

"MAXITO, MAXITO, MAXITO!" Bellita texted. "I cannot wait long to see you."

Naturally, a warm sensation came over me that I cannot describe. It was the same one I got when I spent time at Casa Velasco. It was similar to my emotions when Diana kissed me during the Bacalar rain. And that's when it hit me. What Milo and I lacked was love—or, at the least, a bond and chemistry that was deeper than a physical connection. Even though I liked having sex with Milo, my heart echoed through my body that there wasn't anything meaningful left to explore. It deserved much better than that. Maybe, I encouraged this toxic behavior with Milo—pretending we got back the spark from our youth to compensate for the relationships in my life I didn't pay attention to enough. Maybe, being desperate for "love" can make people do things they regret. Before I led Milo on further, he needed to understand what my plans were.

"Someone in my family is sick and I need to go to Mexico City tonight," I said, pulling away from his lips. "I know...I know it's last minute, but I also need to be there for my cousi —"

"Great joke, brother...but you're not going anywhere," Milo snapped. "Just do me now."

"But... I'm not lying, though. My family needs me in Mexico City with them. And I'm using one of my paid days off,

so I'll be back at work Tuesday. Sorry, I didn't really mean to
—"

"After everything I've done for you?" Milo said, visibly
upset. "Wow, brother. First, you embarrass the hell out of me on
New Year's. And now this? Tell me, who do you think you
are?"

"No, who the hell do you think you are?" I said, feeling
Milo's rage grow stronger. "I just told you someone in my
family got covid and I'm using the day off to travel. Fuck, man,
where's your heart? Look, maybe she'll recover fast. I hope that
actually happens. But I still need to go."

"Since when are you this caring, though?" Milo said,
condescendingly. "Forget them! There's a chance you'll get
covid, too, if you go see your family or whatever the fuck you'll
do."

"Excuse me?" I said, offended. "All I'll be doing is praying
for a good recovery."

"Bullshit. You just want to leave me," Milo said. "You can
pray literally anywhere."

"No, wait... I don't get you. Why do you think I'd leave
you for no reason—"

"Yeah, yeah. Just tell me where you went after you ditched
me in Bacalar," Milo said. "Did your family have covid then as
well? It must've been a 'good recovery' because I didn't even
hear about it. You didn't speak or cry to anyone. Well, at least
nobody I don't fucking know."

That stumped me. I wasn't sure what Milo implied. But
after, Milo pulled me close and kissed me as though I'd vanish
forever if he let me go. He grabbed me with a force that got me
to realize something: he cared more to keep me in his life than
loving me with all his heart. He didn't want to build a
relationship because he figured that paying my salary was
enough for my happiness. Starting with the feature article I
wrote of him back at university, I was a muse which reminded
Milo his dreams were possible. But his vision for us now was
unrealistic fantasies.

"Listen, brother, I'm sorry for the way I'm reacting," Milo said with intensity in his eyes. "I just don't like the idea of losing you. I guess a part of me still feels like I'm in high school with you by my side. You make me feel normal, and it's hard these days with my fame and shit. Please, don't go yet. The video from Bacalar is going to be fully edited by Thursday, so just leave after it drops. Your relative will be okay until then, trust me. Covid isn't that bad, for real."

Milo started to kiss me again. Before things went on longer, I stopped him.

"It's already done," I said, gently pushing him off me. "You don't know shit about what may or may not happen, dude. And I'm sorry... but I can't take this bullshit with you anymore."

"What can't you take, brother?" Milo said, about to laugh. "I've given you so much. You were lost and unemployed when we reconnected. So, tell me, what's the fucking problem now?"

"I don't love you," I said, catching Milo off guard by the look on his face. "Ever since day one... you've shamelessly portrayed this image on social media that we were a thing or more than friends, and we *are* good friends now, but do I love you? Will we ever settle down? Will we ever be anything? No. Sorry if I'm coming off harsh, but it seems like you have feelings, and I don't know what to do with them. Maybe it's my fault for sleeping with you, but still. I'm sorry."

Milo remained quiet for a while. But before long, he started to get dressed. He avoided eye contact the entire time he did. Looking back, he was trying to hide his pain. I didn't feel bad.

"Okay then," Milo said, once fully clothed. "Go to Mexico City or whatever. But if you don't hold off on it until Thursday... watch what'll happen, you ungrateful piece of shit. You can be replaced in a week. Probably less because you're so inexperienced! Do you understand that?"

What scared me most was the fact Milo continued to avoid eye contact. It was as though Milo didn't want to admit I killed his fantasy. It was like my face represented his broken dreams.

"I'll be back Tuesday," I said. "But just not in Cancun. I need to make sure everyone in my family is okay. No worries, though. Since I work on my laptop, I won't miss any deadlines."

"You picked the wrong time to fuck with my emotions like that," Milo said in tears. "I'll make you pay, brother, and it'll cost you more than just money. I'll make your peace suffer too."

"Trust me, seeing my family beat covid is all the 'peace' I'll ever need—"

"Get out before I ruin your life!" Milo yelled viciously, forcing me to head for the door.

After leaving Milo's room, I checked the time. It was past 6:30 p.m. and beginning to get dark outside. Considering my flight was set for tomorrow, it seemed like a good time to tell Diana my plans. That night, I messaged her without expecting much in return. I knew we were both drunk on New Year's Eve. And I couldn't ask her to come with me to Mexico City just like that—no matter how strongly we promised things to each other under *las estrellas de Bacalar*. After twenty minutes of no response, I figured we were as hopeless as the pipe dreams Milo had for our relationship. But when I got to my hotel room, I received a text that changed my mood.

"Nooo, don't leave Cancun," Diana texted. "Before you need to see a new friend."

"Okay, that sounds good to me!" I texted back. "What do you have in mind?"

"Come near the lobby in 30 minutes." Diana wrote. "*Tengo surpresas* for you."

Around 7:00 p.m., I came down to see Diana holding a pair of car keys. She had a radiant smile when she told me her friend at a neighboring hotel loaned it to us for the night. It was the start of what felt like an exciting adventure. Suddenly, I forgot about Milo and his bitter outrage.

Diana drove until we reached *Kukulcan Avenue*—walking distance from the mall of the same name. But in our quiet corner, we found ourselves in the darkest part of the street. Looking into Diana's eyes, it was clear she parked there on purpose. She pulled me until our lips met—grazing them with a burning hint of passion. We felt each other's bodies so much that I felt her heartbeat. Time was irrelevant. It appeared we got sucked into a world that one could only see in a romance novel. It was an instance of bliss, connection, and intimacy—a last night in Cancun to remember. But for every second we made out in that car, I thought of one question: Will she meet me in Mexico City, or was it a beautiful lie? It was hard to know what Diana was thinking.

"*Vamanos,* my friend is at his work," Diana said, turning to open the car door.

"Hold on a minute," I said, gently pulling her back. "We can see your friend—"

"The mall close soon!" Diana said, bizarrely in a rush. "Come before he goes away."

Even though the urgency in Diana's voice caught me off guard, I followed her lead. It almost felt like she was my girlfriend. But now, I realize it was a fantasy that'd never come true.

"Sorry, you're right," I said. "Maybe you know... I just like having you all to myself."

"The world is too big to share with just one," Diana said. "But I do love your sweetness."

Roaming through Place Kukulcan Mall, we explored like children. We checked out stores for minutes at a time. We tried on *sombreros* and laughed at ourselves in the process. It was undeniable our relationship was growing stronger. Honestly, it appeared our energy would never dissipate for those who spotted us. But an hour before the mall closed, we got to a tequila shop.

The first half of the shop carried shelves of different tequilas to choose from, souvenirs that one could find everywhere in Cancun, and a welcoming ambiance that encouraged you to walk through the door. But the other half looked like a fun bar scene that could be rented out for corporate parties or even a small wedding. There were barrels of alcohol surrounding an open area for people to dance. Color, tropical decorations, a few tables, and a counter with stools at the back made for a great setting. That's when Diego emerged, ready to greet us with shots of a store-made tequila. He was short, with nicely combed hair, brown eyes, and an impressive tan. But mostly, I couldn't help feeling attracted to him. You could sense his vibrant energy from the moment he entered a room. He made me excited. It was crazy to experience with Diana around.

After a little conversation, I found out that Diego was of Spaniard descent and moved to Cancun from Mexico City to escape the hectic nature of office life. Unsurprisingly, Diego was also a social media content creator with 800,000 followers on TikTok as the "Tequila King". There was something charming about him. It kept me engaged in whatever he had to say that night. His sales ability and online persona made him great with people. He was a showman who never stopped going. But at the same time, he didn't make me feel pressured to buy something or overwhelmed by the kind of upbeat energy most influencers have. No, I felt relaxed and at ease when he poured us samples to drink and played salsa music. Diego got out of the rat race fifteen years ago, and never looked back—choosing "love over comfort" as he proudly described it, until he found a home in Cancun. He was full of purpose. Better yet, Diego didn't have regrets.

"Look over here…tequila is a world," Diego said, enthusiastically practicing his English in our conversation. "You ever read Paolo Coelho books? He inspire me to follow my destiny, *mi camino por el futuro*. When you recognize the omens, your life changes. You will begin to see and discover love. So, that is why I drink tequila. It is my love and one I must share *con todos*."

Right then, Diego poured three more shots and moved to the salsa music playing subtly in the background. His body hypnotized me in a way I couldn't hide, which got Diana to notice. She didn't say a word yet gave me funny little smirks. And somehow, I knew what they meant.

"So, how long have you known Diana?" I asked him. "I'm curious, honestly."

"*Dios mio*, I don't recall," Diego said, laughing. "Maybe two years or more?"

"More time, *wey,*" Diana said, lightly hitting his arm. "Remember we meet in Playa?"

"Oh, *si, si, si*," Diego said, nodding his head along with his pointer finger before turning to face me again. "We meet as Diana was the waitress at the *restaurante* I go to for...*olvide, pero si*, I was there for a bachelor party. It is where I discover Coelho for first time and became more excited for all the unknowns, *sabes*? Playa is amazing, *hermano*, so much fun. But, eh...*cómo dices*... three or four years after this, I move to Cancun, and open *mi tienda*. I have seen Diana in Cancun too many times since then and she reminds me the good omens are everywhere. I also love that Diana follows hers, too, with photography. She also say to me you like writing stories?"

"Yeah... content for Joie Media mostly. But sometimes, I write creative stuff."

"Keep on going this path," Diego said, pouring more shots and giving Diana weird looks. "Always be true to...where you are and who you are to be, *mi amigo*. With no stories, I don't live in Cancun. They inspire me to go from a bad office and to follow *mi corazon*. I love *los Mayas, y porque soy Español originalmente*, the very beginnings of how Mexico started to be is fascinating for me. We unite for drinks, *fútbol*, tacos, *familia*, women, and good times. Even if it was never always like this in the history of Mexico, the omens eventually brought us to smile."

"Always I love the philosophies you have," Diana said, playfully hitting his arm.

"I miss you each time you are not here with me," Diego said passionately in Spanish, placing her hand on his chest. For some reason, I became jealous of the affection Diego gave her.

"Yes, I agree," I jumped in, disrupting their moment. "I like your philosophies too."

Both looked at me startled as if they forgot I was sitting next to them. It appeared I was an outsider looking into their world—making it awkward. That forced Diego to change subjects.

"So, will you like to buy?" Diego asked, politely. *"Bahosh por tequila, verdad?"*

"Wait, sorry... *que dijiste?*" I said, caught off guard by the wording.

He laughed.

"Bahosh in Mayan is 'how much' in English and in Spanish," Diego said with pride.

"Oh... *que padre,*" I said, turning to look at Diana while she continued to stare at Diego. I never asked what their situation was, yet a scary thought came into my head. Was he one of the ex-lovers' *mis primos* warned me about at Casa Velasco? Quietly, I began to wonder if Diana ever saw Diego on all the days she'd be nowhere to be found. Maybe Diana loved Cancun because of him? I had so many questions. "I learned something new tonight, so *muchas gracias.*"

"Embrace the omens," Diego said, raising his shot glass. "Diana say you're Mexican?"

"Believe it or not, yeah!" I said, drinking my third shot. *"Pero, nací en Canada."*

"I believe this," Diego said with a smile. "I like that you have cultures inside you. And now you have more since you learn Mayan. Continue to grow. We have just one life, *tu entiendes?*"

"See, that's why I introduced you," Diana said, her eyes twinkling with excitement. "Diego was once lost and didn't know what he likes. But now, he's amazing. And you can be this also."

"Vale, que cierto. You can live well," Diego said, retrieving a small bottle of tequila from the shelf behind him. "Take for the roads, *mi amigo Canadiense.* It is my gift from the universe."

"Wait, are you sure about that?" I said as Diego firmly placed the bottle in my hand.

"No pasa nada! All I ask is for a return with DJ Milo Joie and other celebrities. This is my hope *para mi tienda.* And since you and Diana are connected, it is a good omen. Share the word.

Be part of my destined path for the nearby future and I will reward you with even better gifts."

Once Place Kukulcan closed for the night, we headed back to Diana's car ready to seek the omens. With Diego in mind, I thought of what the universe wanted me to recognize. What did it mean to be with Diana that particular evening? But it was then she decided to turn on the radio. Salsa music played—similar to the rhythms and sounds back at Diego's tequila shop. We rolled down the windows, began to drive faster, and embraced the roads of Cancun like they were ours. Soon enough, we both sang with passion. I got the feeling it made the universe smile.

But despite our moment, there was a lot between us that wasn't being said. I realized I didn't know Diana as well as I thought. And it needed to change. The way Diego loved tequila was how I wanted to love Diana. It's how I prayed she would love me in return. Maybe that was an omen? Diego's spiritual presence was captivating. But how effortlessly Diana was drawn to him made me wonder about her feelings for him. Did they ever have a relationship? All these unanswered questions gave me the impression Diana was hiding something. But yet, I also didn't want to let my bullshit ruin whatever we had. That's what made what she told me next feel more special.

"I come to Mexico City to see you. Mexico, Puerto Rico, Miami, *Europa, el mundo...* let's see everywhere together," Diana said, cracking a beautiful smile that held an intoxicating energy. "And let us be true in this life. I bring you to Diego to inspire you because his story reminds me of you. But since Bacalar, we should explore more. I know you like Milo and also Diego from what I see, but that is fine. Love is complex, that is what makes it interesting. And I realize that if you go, I'd like to follow... *quiero todo que yo puedo contigo.* I want happiness *para siempre.*"

Naturally, I didn't know how to respond. But yet, the courage Diana had to say what she did meant the world to me. She wanted to take a chance on our love, a risk on why we choose to love the ones we do. Even with all that happened later, I'll always cherish her heart for those words.

"I've never known anyone like you," I said. "And I don't plan to ever again."

"And I never before like someone *como las estrellas,*" Diana said, rubbing my leg.

"Honestly, I...I want Mexico, you, and nothing else," I said, barely able to control myself.

Minutes later, Diana parked the car in front of the Oasis hotel.

"Let's go," Diana said, leaning over to kiss me softly. "I hear *las estrellas* calling."

Before long, Diana insisted we go around the Oasis until we reached a back entrance to the beach used by resort staff. Looking back, I don't know what Diana was hiding from. But as I held Diana's hand and walked until we couldn't see the light from the Oasis, it didn't matter. I took out the small tequila Diego gave me, and we drank the further we strolled. Eventually, we got tipsy and began to dance along to the sounds of the ocean. I never felt so connected with another human like I did then. This was our dream come true—the Mayans were singing to us.

After what seemed like an eternity, Diana and I found a spot that overlooked the moon. Everything in the world disappeared —jobs, COVID-19, Milo, and even the future. Hope and anticipation of what might happen next are what remained. Slowly, our clothes began to peel off. Her breathing intensified when I placed my hands on her breasts. Making love in an intimate setting like the beach in Cancun was terrifying, but we gave in to what we believed the universe wanted us to do. It was the best sex I ever had. And something told me that Diana felt the same.

Chapter 15

January 16, 2022

Suddenly, my work-life balance was nonexistent. It was impossible to have a life outside Joie Media anymore. From the moment Tuesday came around, Milo changed my schedule from 10:00-6:00 p.m. to 8:00-6:00 p.m. with an additional block of 8:00-5:00 p.m. on Saturdays. From what Milo and the editorial team described to me Tuesday morning, I was now assigned extra hours to do customer service—a time-consuming effort replying to emails and DMs of every person who didn't get merch on time, got the wrong T-shirt size, or had a problem with a hyperlink on Joie Media's website. It was all a pointless headache that didn't even come with a pay raise and no extra benefits. Looking back, Milo wanted me to struggle mentally. But when I asked people on the editorial team about my customer service duties, they all said it was a "great opportunity to build more skills in my career". It was a corporate response that lacked emotions.

Despite most people at Joie Media were off the clock on the weekend, it seemed my life was now about work, work, and more work. I went from having occasional two-hour lunch breaks to just thirty minutes. Milo sentenced me to death without saying the words. Back then, I didn't get why nobody called him out on his toxic behavior. Maybe people loved that I wasn't getting special treatment anymore. Besides, nobody else at Joie Media got big lunch breaks, fun day trips to *Chichén Itza*, Milo's vote of confidence, and a good job title at a prestigious company like Milo's without any prior credits on their resume. It's fair to assume I beat out hundreds of candidates who probably deserved my job a lot more, yet never even got an interview. Maybe I was ungrateful? But that also didn't stop me from realizing Joie Media was full of corporate assholes who considered me "family" at Milo's expense, since he paid their salaries.

Before I ended our "meet-ups", I used to feel comfortable talking to my editors about content ideas for Joie Media's blog and social media pages. Pitching new stuff and the creative process of doing so in a professional environment was a passion of mine. Better yet, I even used to make my co-workers laugh during our biweekly check-in meetings. But in the last week, I started to get harsher notes on my blog articles, social media posts, and even how I'd interacted with Milo's followers in customer service. There was more negative feedback in a week than I received in all the months working for Joie Media combined. But then, a scary thought came to mind: maybe he knew. Maybe the relationship I built with Diana in quiet moments was no longer a secret to anyone. And maybe Milo was devastated, taking out his frustration on me somehow.

Regardless, though, something was off. Once I texted Milo about how difficult my new hours were and how I wasn't even trained to do customer service, he replied with: "A new contract means new responsibilities and higher expectations, brother." It seemed condescending. But, although I'd sometimes log off work after 6:30 p.m., Milo and people from my team would often say nice things like "good job" or "thanks for your hard work". I remember being confused by their messaging, considering all my bad notes. But I also let it go, happy for the time to rest.

The worst thing about my new hours was exactly that. If I didn't make good use of my morning, I'd be working away until the day was gone. Even though I was at Casa Velasco with *mis primos, tio, y tia*, most of my time was spent in their guestroom from the moment I arrived. If I was lucky, I enjoyed coffee with them at 7:30 a.m., laughed, talked, and caught up on what was going on in their lives until I had to lock myself in that room with my laptop until dinner. It was a miserable week. Every time

I went to bed late, I'd wake up and head straight to work. If by some miracle I'd get a proper eight hours and be up around 7:00 a.m., I'd stress about the work that was to come. It appeared like Milo wanted me to suffer, to quit my job, to feel what he felt. But along with that pressure, there were more important things to worry about at Casa Velasco.

Abuela Velasco was having a really difficult time battling COVID-19 and had to be hospitalized. Every night after dinner, we'd all gather to pray—hoping to the Gods above that Abuela Velasco would make a full recovery. Hugo, Sara, and Manuel were coughing. Jose, although recovered from COVID-19, was still a little weak. Thankfully for us, Clarisa used her skills and knowledge as a nurse to take care of Abuela Velasco. But that also meant Clarisa had the greatest chance of being infected since she was around sick patients over thirty-five hours a week. Looking back, perhaps being trapped at work saved me from testing positive in that brief period. After all, I only went from my room, the kitchen, and the bathroom. But I came to learn the hard way you should never underestimate the pandemic. Nobody was immune to being sick.

Throughout the week I was in Mexico City, Bellita was by far the most shaken by the whole thing. She missed her *abuela* like crazy and prayed at the dinner table harder than anyone else. Everyone at the house played games with her, and there were friends of hers from dance classes and the *taqueria* who came over. But it all seemed pointless until her *abuela* returned home.

Even with emotions running high, it was nice to get a text from Diana Saturday morning that she was in Mexico City. She was going to stay with a friend in *La Condesa*, a popular gem of a neighborhood that was home to a variety of good restaurants, people, and two famous parks—*Parque México y Parque España*. It was also close to *La Roma* and *El Castillo de Chapultepec*.

On that Saturday morning, just before 8:00 a.m., I decided to book another day off in the Joie Media system. With Diana on my mind, all I wanted to do was take a beautiful walk with her in Parque Mexico. But I also thought of getting Bellita to tag along that afternoon. After all, there was nobody more likable in the world than Bellita. If she gave me her stamp of approval, I'd know Diana was my destined "Falcon love". I'd know we were meant for happily ever after.

Strangely, despite the intense week, none of my coworkers seemed to care when I requested time off. Milo didn't attack me in an email or a call, which really surprised me because I expected it to happen. But Milo's video team finished editing a wonderful piece from the footage shot at the New Year's Eve party in Bacalar. It ended up dropping on Friday and got a storm of online attention. I was so busy with my job that I never even watched the video. And since I wasn't with Milo that much anymore, I figured there was no reason for me to care how it looked. Maybe I would've had a lot to explain to Diana if I was shown kissing Milo in Bacalar. It would've gone viral. But, considering our late-night talk in Cancun before the beach, I felt safe. Nobody would cyberbully me about my sexuality. Nobody in my family would be taken aback.

From what I heard, most people enjoyed the good vibes Milo encouraged in the video, the party, and the overall sense of uplifting energy he wanted to symbolize for better days to come based on the comments, likes, and shares. Granted, others also hated the video, criticized Milo's lack of respect for the pandemic rules, and left strongly worded messages for him to read. Both sides made valid points, yet Milo's video got 500,000 clicks in less than twenty-four hours and was deemed a successful project. Looking back, that statistic made me feel better about taking another day off to put a smile on Bellita's face. I needed a work-life balance somewhere.

* * * *

"Want to go to the park?" I said to Bellita during breakfast Saturday morning as she wrote in the notebook gifted to her by my mother. "I remember we haven't gone yet, so *que tu piensas*?"

"No working today or what you do?" Bellita said, looking up with surprise.

"Yes, no trabajo hoy!" I smiled. "So, would you like to go with me later?"

"Claro que si!" Bellita shut her notebook. "I don't want you alone there."

Everyone at the house that morning was busy with something or needed to be at *la taqueria*. Despite having barely recovered from COVID-19, Jose was more enthusiastic than he's ever been to keep his restaurant alive. In fact, he asked me to bring Bellita home before dinner so she could get ready for work later that evening. Looking back, everyone at Casa Velasco was just as invested in their careers as I was at the time. But yet, family was at the center of everything they did—that's how they achieved balance. We all gathered to pray together before Clarisa left for the hospital, asking God to spare Abuela Velasco for many years to come. But after everyone got on with their day, it seemed that Bellita and I had forever to see what Mexico City had to offer.

"Vamos después breakfast,*"* I said, making her light up with positive energy.

"It will be so amazing," Bellita said. She did a little dance as she got up to head toward the kitchen sink to clean up her breakfast dish. "I love today already. *Me encanta mis dias contigo.*"

When the morning faded into the afternoon, we were off to explore *La Condesa*. We strolled happily from Parque Mexico to Parque España, and then around La Roma close to where El Castillo de Chapultepec was located. I bought her fish tacos for lunch at one of the great restaurants in the neighborhood. And we met some new friends when a group of Canadian expats asked us for directions to a café. Eventually, though, we found ourselves in an interesting area of Parque Mexico. It was a giant open space with white floor tiles circularly fashioned. Outlining the white tiles were endless benches to sit on. But overlooking it was a Roman-like architecture.

Children passed around a *futbol* in the open space, people walked with their families, some vendors wandered through, and others even ate lunch on the benches. It was chaotic, yet also full of life. Everything coexisted somehow, and it portrayed to me at that moment Mexico's spirit—crazy, imperfect, raw, and beautiful all at once. But even while I took in that environment with Bellita sitting next to me, I kept checking my phone to see if Diana was close to us at the park.

"*Dime,* because I'm curious now… what's your favorite thing about *El Castillo de Chapultepec*?" I asked Bellita as we sat on a bench that overlooked the Roman-like architecture. "I read about the history, and I find it so intriguing. I didn't know European royalty lived there."

"I like how they have many rooms in *El Castillo*!" Bellita said. "You can make food, play games, sleep, and do everything you choose in lots of spaces. It is cool, no? What do you think?"

"Yes, *tienes razón*! But I also find it kind of funny that we can see where those kings and queens used to sleep at night. Imagine millions of people each year seeing your bed, am I right?"

"So truthful*, primo,*" Bellita said, laughing. "I don't like even when *abuela* see mine."

All of a sudden, Bellita's mood changed. Tears rose to the border of her eyelids. Emotionally, it crushed me as I thought of how Abuela Velasco was doing. And that's what led me to ask more questions, to create banter, anything to help Bellita continue enjoying our day together. Deep inside, I prayed for the best. The world lacked meaning without a Bellita smile.

"So, tell me something… what kind of room would you like in your own house?"

"*Postres, postres, postres!*" Bellita said, after a pause. "A room for desert and good treats."

"*Como una panadería?*" I asked, while Bellita looked at me with a fire I didn't expect.

"*Si, Maxito!*" Bellita said. "I think so much, and I believe that I want to start a bakery, *una panadería*, someplace where I can make things I love and share with each person. I love, love, love also *la taqueria*, but I need to follow what I'd want. Even if I can't do this dream now."

Honestly, it was the first time I ever heard Bellita speak like that. I did know she loved to bake with her grandmother in their little apartment, yet never realized she had that ambition. It made me think of Diego for a second. Maybe, there were many sides to Bellita I never met. She had a whole life before I even got to Mexico. And there was a lot about what made Bellita who she was that I'd never understand. She had so much to share with people, her family, the world. But I also wondered if I would've found out about Bellita's quiet hopes sooner if I made more of an effort to stay in touch with her the last decade. Deep down, I was feeling ashamed of that reality in my life—I should've valued family more, regardless of where they lived. But I felt the passion in Bellita's voice. I wanted to encourage her to dream big. I wanted her to succeed.

"Wait, so… how long have you had this vision, anyway?" I asked with interest.

"I don't know for how much time, but I like *dulces* and I like people," Bellita replied, cheerfully. The more we talked, the more her confidence grew. "I want them to be happy, always, and great ways to do this is by giving them food. I never see any person upset with that."

"Do you have a name for your *panaderia*?" I asked. "And does everyone know?"

"No, because I don't want them to make fun," Bellita said. "But I realize my parents know…who knows where they are, but they are proud. They look at me from below and smile."

"Why do you think?" I asked, feeling inspired by Bellita's optimism. "Tell me more."

"I hope to do this *con mi abuela*," Bellita said, after a long pause. "She teached *mi mama* to create *postres* and she then teach it to me. I will carry forward their love, as they say *en ingles*. And I want them to understand that I remember. I remember their *corazón* because I have it too."

Right then, Bellita's face lit up with a spark of happiness. I wanted to hug her, yet I felt it wasn't the best move. I just sat quietly, supporting *mi prima* until she was ready to speak again.

"I know they'll be so proud of you," I said, watching her tuck a loose strand of hair behind her ear. "It's what I am now. And if you believe, you can achieve everything that you dream."

"Mamita Velasco!" Bellita said, bursting with pride. "I can't think of any better names."

"Neither can I when it comes to *panaderias*. And I really want to visit yours."

Bellita looked at me like I said everything she hoped to hear. She reached for my hand, and I grabbed hold of it tightly. Reflecting on this now, I don't believe there's ever been a shared moment that was so perfect as right now. I gave her the gift of encouragement. I gave Bellita the confidence to accomplish things. I didn't want our day to end. But then, I got a text from Diana.

"What you read?" Bellita asked, seeing I was glued to my phone. "I like reading, too, so can you tell me what is this? I love the memes and the fun videos. Are you looking at these things?"

"No. It's just my friend is close by," I said, while I scanned everyone by the white tiles.

"Okay," Bellita said, looking straight at the ground. "I wait for you to see her then."

"Todo bien?" I asked, feeling confused. "Sorry, didn't I say a friend was meeting us?"

"Never," Bellita said. "I think it is our time now. Why do you ask others to come?"

The radiance and emotion painted on Bellita's face throughout the day had disappeared. Our moment was ruined. It faded with every step Diana took toward the white tiles and the Roman-like architecture. Bellita didn't cry, yet I felt her disappointment. It caught me off guard because she often loved meeting new people. But what I didn't realize back then was just how much Bellita valued our quality time together. She knew that Jose would soon call her into work at *la tacquiera*. She also knew I had my job and didn't do much else. It was important for Bellita to have a day with me because she adored her family, friends, and the little things which make life great. Inviting

Diana into our space was a mistake—more than Bellita's heart could take. I understand now. But at the time, I couldn't figure out the problem. I wish I could repeat things.

Minutes later, Diana got to the white tiles. She wore a pair of ripped jeans, a sweater, and held a purse. It was a more laid-back look than what I remembered in the months we knew each other. But as she got closer to where we happened to be, I noticed something else—a mask. She took it off to greet me briefly with a kiss on the cheek and a hug. But she placed it back on her face soon after. It appeared like Diana might've had a cold. It made me question why she came.

"*Hola, hola,*" Diana said, pausing to cough. "No worries, I'm fine. I can still be here."

"Wait, are you sure?" I asked, noticing Bellita's concerned expression.

"Sorry, I do not feel very good. I don't know why, but the air will get me better."

From the instant Diana reached us, I should've known. It had to be what I thought it was. But I chose not to question things. I didn't have the guts to turn away someone I thought I loved.

"So, what are you both doing today?" Diana asked, before coughing into her arm.

"Everything," Bellita said, grabbing my hand. You could tell she was uncomfortable by the way she talked to Diana. She even gave me a sharp look which indicated she wanted to leave. "Eating, walking, speaking, and also we laugh. It's very nice to be outside. We enjoy so much."

"I feel that we should capture it forever then," Diana said, taking out her phone from her purse before moving toward me. "It does sound like fun. And I want to be very much included."

Naturally, Diana smiled at Bellita and tried to hand over her phone. Looking back, it was rude on Diana's part. She just wanted to give off the illusion she was with us that whole time. I should've told Diana off, yet I didn't for whatever reason. Bellita, on the other hand, became red.

"Why do you come and pretend you like Maxito for Instagram?" Bellita asked, on the verge of crying. "You take him away from me and this really makes me not so happy. *Dime, porque?*"

"I love being with him," Diana said to Bellita in Spanish. "Those are my reasons."

"No, you pretend and that is not nice!" Bellita said with tears streaming down her face. "I know what your colors are. You date friends of people in my family and in my work, and you do this often. You act like you love and then go away. You'll hurt Max and that gives me sadness."

"Max invited me, so don't you start," Diana said in Spanish. "You don't know anything."

Right then, I got a text from Jose. He asked me to begin heading back to Casa Velasco.

"Hey, it seems like we need to leave soon, anyway," I said, showing Bellita my phone so she could read Jose's text. "So, maybe taking a few photos to capture this moment isn't a bad idea?"

"Yes, that is what I try to say," Diana said, handing Bellita her phone once again. It was evident Bellita was still upset, but I gave her a quick hug and reassured her we'd be home soon.

"Fine, I take the pictures for you," Bellita said, after a long pause.

When Bellita took Diana's phone, I felt good again knowing Diana was by my side. She took Bellita's place on the bench and pulled me closer as though we'd been dating for years. It resulted in some beautiful results that Diana posted—gaining about fifty likes in twenty minutes. Gathering all together, we then took a selfie of the three of us. It was by far the greatest one—so much so that Bellita asked Diana to send the photo to her so she could send it to her *abuela*. She also wanted me to help her make it her Facebook profile picture. Finally, her tears were gone.

"Anyway, I know a bar near here if you want to drink," Diana said, coughing again. She looked at me like I was the only person in all of Mexico. "Want to go with me and my friends?"

"No way. Maxito needs to come with me first," Bellita said, giving me another look that indicated she wanted to go home, tugging at my shirt without stopping. "Drink in another time."

Tensions were high between Diana and Bellita. But I stepped in before things escalated.

"Maybe later," I answered. "I'll just drop Bellita off and then meet you afterward."

"Orale!" Diana took off her mask to kiss me on the cheek once again. "I'll send you the address, okay? It is about... a thirty-minute walk close to here. I'll save you *glasses de mezcal.*"

After a short wait, the Uber arrived and brought us back home. I didn't know what could've been said the whole ride, even if my life depended on it. But once we got out of the Uber and walked toward our front door, I opened my mouth. I wanted to make sure we were okay.

"Sorry, Bellita, I probably shouldn't have asked Diana to join us," I said, as genuinely as I could. "I promise that I'll never do that again. I love you, *te quiero.* And...please, forgive me."

Bellita stared at me for what seemed like an endless period. You could tell she was still recovering from her fight with Diana. It made me regret bringing her even more. But when I least expected it, Bellita took my hand and cracked a smile. It was the type that could end wars.

"If you love her dearly...then I accept her as well." She gave me a warm hug. "I do not care for her. I believe she is not great for you and all the nice people I know. But if it is a love that is dear and for real, I want you to have this love. It is because love is all that I truly want for you."

"Gracias, prima," I said, feeling her warmth as she continued to hold me without letting go. She was the most beautiful person I've ever met. Her approval meant the world to me—more than I'd ever know when I reflected on things later. That hug and that day would forever be ours.

"With pleasure," Bellita said, while we stood in front of Casa Velasco. "Now go and see if this love you have is for real with Diana. And I... I will also chase love too *con mi panaderia*."

Later that night, I found myself at a rooftop bar with Diana and a couple of her friends. It was hard not to think about the kindness Bellita gave me while I drank shots of mezcal. Better yet, it got me to question what it meant to love anything in life. She had more grace than most people. Her emotional intelligence was vast and immeasurable. Despite these thoughts in the back of my mind, however, I was having a good time. I drank more than necessary, socialized with Diana's friends and gained a handful of new Instagram followers. But just when I started to relax, I got a notification that made my heart sink. All of a sudden, it brought me down to earth.

"Wow, thank GOD everyone is healthy," Milo wrote in the comment section of Diana's post. He followed this with laughing face emojis and three periods at the end. It made me shiver.

Chapter 16

January 19, 2022

Even though Milo's response to Diana's photo of us was passive-aggressive, he seemed okay when I asked him about everything later. I believed Milo was at ease, regretting the way he commented on that post. The last few days were bizarre, especially when I developed flu-like symptoms. I figured that I caught something minor from Diana. It was, after all, the cold season in Mexico, so it made sense to me on paper. But I didn't allow Milo or my health to affect my work performance. I didn't want to believe I had COVID-19. That would have been a nightmare.

Reflecting back on things now, Milo was beginning to accept that we'd never be in a relationship, have a future together as more than colleagues, or get remotely close to the happily ever after he wanted. He even complimented me on two blogs I did that week. It was a good confidence booster since it didn't seem as though other companies liked me for whatever reason.

The fake-politeness many businesses exhibited in their "culture" made the rejections in my inbox more depressing to handle. I made it to the final round of interviews with a marketing agency that "believed" I was the right fit, connected with the CEO on LinkedIn, yet still received a bullshit form letter. I also made it to the second round of interviews at a start-up yet found myself being ghosted. Another company "was touched" by the sample pieces I submitted with my job application one minute, yet three days later, sent me a heartless rejection. I kept getting so close, yet not close enough to land a job offer. It was tiring to constantly read the words "not a good fit at this time" and "we encourage you to check our careers page for future opportunities".

For over a month, I had no idea why people applied to hundreds of corporate jobs—sometimes for a year—with the hopes of landing just one. It was probably for the high salary, the position in society, and the respect from your peers. But it seemed like a frivolous pursuit unless you were a CEO or a top employee in an organization. Everyone else was struggling to make it.

Suddenly, I began to accept the idea of moving up the corporate ladder at Joie Media. To my great surprise, I even hoped to gain the title of "Senior Editor" if everything went according to plan. Inspiration came from realizing how impossible it was to get employed. I was lucky to know Milo and that he became a famous DJ. But just when I thought life couldn't have been so bad if I continued to stay with Milo, an email popped up in my inbox that made my heart pound.

"Hey Max,

Hope all is good. You have a feedback evaluation at 4:00 p.m., so please do not forget.
Looking forward to speaking, brother.

Cheers,
-Milo."

What was a feedback evaluation? The term sounded confusing, and a little scary to read based on the dryness from Milo's tone of writing. For a minute or two, I thought the worst. Maybe some of my blog articles and social media posts weren't on brand. But it was 3:15 p.m. at that point, so it was impossible not to be nervous. I recall getting up from my desk to pace around, coughing and feeling lightheaded, freaking out even more. All of a sudden, a terrible headache developed, and my throat dried up with each inhale of breath. Maybe it was stress from all the hours I worked. But a co-worker eased me somewhat when I asked him about the email.

"Sometimes, that's just what bosses do. It's normal and to be expected," Michael said, a new senior editor that worked alongside Jennifer. Funny enough, he was one of three new hires that week. Michael was the type of person who'd ghost you over email, and then complain if you didn't answer him immediately. He was quiet, cold, a robot when it came to following orders—a company's dream. "Don't worry too much about it, okay? Focus on your work. Based on what I've seen, I think you're doing well. Keep improving on your craft and developing your skills."

Maybe it was Joie Media's protocol? I did sign a new contract, so it might've been "normal" to have my progress "evaluated" on a regular basis. Or perhaps, they were checking in to make sure I was doing okay. Besides, working from 8:00-6:00 p.m. with lots of unpaid overtime could damage anyone's mental health if they weren't too careful. I thought Milo cared about my career success and I was surrounded by a "family" that loved having me on their team.

In the brief time I worked under the new schedule, I didn't have much of a life. After closing my laptop for the day, I only had time for dinner, a few rounds of Connect Four with Bellita, and, if I was lucky, an episode of a television show before I needed to sleep. I was burning out.

Despite it having only been two weeks, it was harder to concentrate. I woke up hating the blog writing tasks I used to enjoy. I felt stuck with Milo, yet excited to move up the corporate ladder. I didn't know who I was anymore. But that is when Jose knocked on my bedroom door.

"Ven a bajo," Jose said with a sad look in his eyes. "I know you working but come."

When I got downstairs, Bellita was being consoled by Hugo and Sara. I saw Manuel trying to control his tears, and Clarisa trying her best to remain strong. Something was not right.

"I spoke with the doctors," Jose said. "They say *abuela* is having many troubles."

Bellita sobbed even more.

"We cannot be in the room with her at the hospital," Jose continued. "But we should be in the building. She need us close. We pray first *y vamos después*. Let's hope she recovers well."

Around 3:45 p.m., everyone prepared to leave—even Jose, which surprised me considering what he'd been through. It showed leadership in my opinion because a hospital was the last place he should've gone. But yet, he chose to go anyway for someone he loved. It all happened so quickly that I found myself at a crossroads. Do I skip the "feedback evaluation" and just reschedule? Do I miss this family moment for responsibilities at work? I also wasn't sure if it was the greatest idea since I felt sick and didn't want to spread it around. Confusion whirled.

But, on the other hand, the "feedback evaluation" appeared important. It might've been Abuela Velasco's final hours, yet I thought of what everyone at Joie Media would think. I'm still ashamed. I told myself people survived COVID-19 all the time. So, why couldn't *abuela*? Everyone knew she was a strong woman compared to most. I believed that with all my heart.

"Hey, I'll meet you guys there," I said, turning my phone to everyone. "*Tengo* un meeting, but it won't take me long. I'll call an Uber when I'm done. I'll pray for *abuela… te prometo*."

There was no doubt *mi familia* was shocked by the look on their faces. But the clock was ticking—Abuela Velasco was waiting for her fate to meet her whether it turned out good or bad.

"Text us when you're in Uber," Jose said, as everyone remained taken by my decision.

After they drove off, I couldn't move without shaking. I hoped to God my team would understand when I told them what was going on in my life. I prayed my "family" at Joie Media would care about me enough to cut the meeting short. That's what I planned to do when I signed into the video call to see the faces of Milo, and two of the senior editors—Jennifer and Michael.

"Having a good day, brother?" Milo asked, calmly with a smile.

"Yeah, I'm just working hard as usual," I said, after a pause. Jennifer and Michael looked at me with poker faces. I didn't know what was coming. But Jennifer reviewed my work for a couple of months prior to this meeting. She liked my job update on LinkedIn when I shared that I got promoted to a permanent copywriter on her team. On the other hand, Michael was new and didn't know me that well. Maybe I was overthinking? That is what I continued to say to myself.

"Oh, same," Milo said. "Look, I'm not going to waste more time. We've all been talking, and I don't think we can keep you on board. I find that your skills aren't up to the level we need, and it doesn't make sense to force things. Before you go, though, we'll read you through the severance package you'll get. Thanks for your hard work, brother, but maybe if you develop your skills more, we will consider you again. Do you have anything to say before we continue?"

Milo said that last part emotionless as though he didn't have any other choice. Suddenly, I couldn't say anything if I tried. Was this a twisted joke? The shock of it all was unimaginable. I went from doing a "good job" to being fired. It made no sense. But one thing did come to mind.

"I just signed a new contract, and… I thought I was doing great work. You even told me recently that I was, so…I don't get it. Can you give me another chance? I promise I'll do better."

"Brother, I've looked at your content, and it's not good enough," Milo said, again without emotion. "I don't see you improving fast. Sometimes it takes years to achieve the quality we're looking for. I mean, there's a reason we only gave you a full-time freelance contract. Less risk."

"That's bullshit because you've called me talented since day one!" I fought to keep my job and anger in check. "Fuck, you've called me that in every single text convo we've ever had. You offered me that permanent role because of that, remember? So, what's the fucking problem—"

"Everyone who works here is talented," Jennifer said, cutting me off. You could tell she took no pleasure in this situation. Dread was painted on her face. "But it doesn't mean they always end up being a good fit. We like to focus on growth at Joie Media. And after some consideration, we think you've grown enough with us and should go on to your next challenge."

"What? But you've all said you wanted me to 'grow' here ever since I got hired?" They looked at me confused when I said that. It was as if they were denying that ever happened based on their complexions. Not only did I call out their fakeness, but I exposed it in that call. Somehow it made me feel worse knowing I embraced it. "And Milo always told me that fam—"

"Yes, and you always will be a part of it," Michael said. "But just because things aren't working out now doesn't mean they won't in the future. We're always open to new copywriters."

I couldn't believe how "fake" the fake-politeness was at that moment. It appeared that love and empathy were lost on the people in my feedback evaluation. But then, Milo cut deep.

"See how it feels, brother?" Milo said. "I know it sucks, but you'll get back on your feet."

"Is…is this about what I said in Cancun?" I asked out of desperation. "I want to be with you, man, I wouldn't lie. It's just in a different way than you thought, and I'm sorry if I came off —"

"No, it's more than just Cancun!" Rage encompassed his demeanor. "We just aren't in love with you. That's business sometimes. It's nothing fucking personal, brother, so calm down."

"He's right, Max, sometimes things aren't really a good fit," Michael said, failing to read the room. "That's what the probationary period is for, you know. It happens to so many people."

"Exactly," Jennifer said. "Trust me, you're not alone. And if you want to discuss this further, I'm more than happy to chat with you via email. I can even see if I know anyone hiring."

"But I just got this permanent role," I repeated, while my phone vibrated in my pocket. "And Milo was never clear about that. I signed for five years. Why are you firing me after two weeks? It makes no sense, I'm sorry. Why even give me the contract if you felt I couldn't live up to the standards? Fuck, I was with you guys for a few months. I flew down to Mexico, for God's sake!"

"I wanted to give you a shot," Milo said. "And I liked a bit of the work you did, just not everything. We need someone better suited for the job. Hopefully, you liked your time with us."

"So, all the nights we spent together meant nothing to you?" I said, noticing I struck a chord judging by Milo's complexion. "What about Chichen Itza? Don't you tell me it was all bad—"

"Maybe before it was nice to reconnect...but unlike you, I'm proud of my worth," Milo said. "I know exactly who I am and what I represent, even though it can be difficult. I built a career off that mentality. But you like to hide, and I deserve better. You can't love someone if they can't even love themselves, you know? That's what I suggest you do. I say this as a friend."

Suddenly, another face popped onto the video call. It was someone from Joie Media's HR department. I knew of them but didn't realize we had HR reps until that feedback evaluation.

"At this time," HR began to read with no emotion. "We're prepared to offer two weeks' pay and a reference letter for your next opportunity. We know that you will get back on your feet..."

Before HR continued to read from the bullshit write-up they had, I noticed Milo couldn't hide his smile. It was like he couldn't wait for me to be gone. The pain of it was indescribable.

"You know, this happened to me, too," Jennifer said, trying her best to be genuine but just making things worse. "Once, I didn't get a job I really wanted. But then, that same magazine gave me a column, and I was hired full-time a year later. So just take it as a learning experience."

Where was my column, I thought? It felt like another dagger went straight to my heart.

"I gave up driving to the hospital to be in this meeting," I heard myself saying to them. "My *abuela* might pass away soon, yet I chose to be here. And I told Milo about it…it's why I took one of my sick days, remember? I've worked so hard and sacrificed a lot. Please, don't do this."

"Yeah, yeah, we've all suffered because of the pandemic," Milo said, rolling his eyes. "But here's the major difference, brother… I don't let it define me. I don't let it affect shit in my life."

"But, Milo, we've been friends since high school," I said, trying to revive our spark in a last-ditch effort to save my job. "Remember the locker room? Remember what we did? Fuck, do you remember the blog articles I wrote for you? Do you remember the moment we talked again in the first wave? Did the last few months mean anything? Please, don't do this to me… I love you—"

"Good luck out there, brother," Milo said, cutting me off aggressively. "You'll get your termination papers over email, along with your severance details in like an hour. See you later!"

Once the feedback evaluation concluded, an unexpected sadness came over me as I got up from my chair. It was almost like I was drunk, yet it wasn't alcohol. I was overcome with failure and misery. The shame of it hit me in the way another person might feel excitement after a tequila shot. Hopelessly, with nowhere to go, it seemed I was having an out-of-body experience.

Nothing I did was good enough. It made me question my career, my decisions last month, and the world's upheaval in 2022. But right when I was about to scream, my phone vibrated once more. I checked it to see one dm, one text message, and one email. The magazine that considered *"Songs of the Mayans"* rejected it because they felt other stories in their slush pile were in better shape. They gave me a word document with notes, which I couldn't bring myself to read if I tried. But if that rejection didn't kill my spirit, the text and dm twisted the knife in my back. Jose texted me to say Abuela Velasco died before they reached the hospital. And Diana DM'd me to say she tested positive for COVID-19. Knowing Bellita was near her weeks earlier, panic coursed through me. I was responsible for that. What if I placed Bellita in danger? And what if something terrible happened to her? Combined with losing my job, the fear made me a hot mess.

Chapter 17

February 14, 2022

The depression of being laid off hit me in waves impossible to control. It was the closest thing I've ever come to experiencing PTSD in my life. That "feedback evaluation" played over and over again in my head. I tried to understand what led it to happen. Sometimes, I'd be okay—making peace that I could move on from Joie Media to something more gratifying, free to get a better job away from Milo, like I originally hoped to do. But every time I applied to new opportunities on LinkedIn in the last few weeks, tears streamed down the border of my eyelids.

The way Milo fired me, it brought me back to where I started in 2020. Jobless, broke, confused, and hopeless in the midst of an ongoing pandemic. But I resented Milo and Joie Media more for taking me away from *mi familia* at a crucial moment when they needed my support. It wasn't something I could make up for since Abuela Velasco was now gone. Since then, everyone at Casa Velasco barely spoke to me. It was as though *mi familia* just wanted me to feel their disappointment. The only person who'd even look at me was Bellita. If it wasn't for our Connect Four matches after dinner, I would've been completely unwelcome. This negative energy led me to take long walks for mental health reasons. It seemed there was no purpose in my life anymore—floating through the world aimlessly with nothing to call my own, getting more depressed as the pandemic continued, and feeling sorry for myself with each person who bragged about career success on my newsfeed. It was hard to deal with that. Social media made it worse.

After all, I kept stalking Milo online like an ex-boyfriend who didn't get the closure he needed. But even then, I hid my setback from *mi familia* in Mexico, my parents in Montreal, my friends, and even my online network by changing the job description in my LinkedIn bio from "Brand Copywriter for Joie Media" to "Copywriter & Experienced Social Media Marketer". I prayed I'd get my life back on track before my tourist visa in Mexico expired in two months. Hopefully, I'd be able to land something in the coming weeks. If not, I'd have no choice but to move in with my parents until finding employment. The pressure was on, while I maintained the act of still having a "job" to everyone at Casa Velasco. I stayed inside my room for long periods.

During the self-imposed confinement, I noticed Bellita was also going through her own personal struggles. Ever since Abuela Velasco died, she began to lose her desire to play Connect Four as time progressed. She didn't dance anymore following her victories. Better yet, it became evident to me she was only playing to maintain our quality time together. I tried my best to be present. But once February hit, everything fell apart. Seeing Bellita deteriorate was a nightmare.

Bellita barely ate, didn't smile or laugh, and never wanted to do much anymore. Abuela Velasco's passing continued to shatter her zest for life. But the worst part was, Bellita lost faith in the world she once loved. I remember each time Jose and Clarisa asked her to come with them to dance class, she would decline. Everyone believed Bellita was just going through a grieving process. Friends of hers from *la tacqueria*, dance class, the market, and even Facebook would come over to the house to bring her gifts. Even her salsa teacher offered his Acapulco condo for the weekend, if that meant putting a smile on Bellita's face. Nobody could bear her depression.

Despite the kindnesses, though, Bellita continued to reject everything and everyone around her. But our family and Bellita's friends refused to give up trying to offer support. Looking back, she was unforgettable. She left a good impression on everyone she ever met. It's why that Saturday morning was so scary when I noticed Bellita was having trouble breathing. She gasped for air from her bedroom, and since I was normally the first person up at Casa Velasco the last two weeks, I got to Bellita before anyone else. I remember walking over to her room with the Connect Four box with the innocent hope of lightening up her mood. Maybe Bellita was just sobbing and hyperventilating. But on that Valentine's Day, she couldn't get out of her bed.

"*Como te sientes?* Are you okay?" I asked Bellita, standing at the edge of her door. "Do you want to play Connect Four? I have plenty of free time now and I'd love to spend it with you —"

"*No me...* I do not feel so well, Maxito," Bellita said in tears. "I don't understand why."

"Should I... do you need my help?" I said, after a long pause. "Do you need me to do—"

"It will be okay, you do nothing," Bellita said with a look in her eyes that made me realize this wasn't good. I hoped that it wasn't what it might've been. "You have work, so... you go."

"I don't have work now." I ran over to grab her hand. She couldn't grip mine back.

That's when I called everyone in Casa Velasco. And thanks to Clarisa, we got Bellita a doctor's appointment an hour later. Thankfully, she used her connections at the hospital, and, unsurprisingly, Bellita was loved by everyone there as well. Back when she was a little kid, she'd help give out warm meals to sick patients. She never failed to charm the doctors with her excitement for life, her dance moves, her smile. Not only was she admitted into the emergency room fast, but every single healthcare professional that knew her also carried the same fear in their eyes Bellita had this morning. They knew she just lost her *abuela*. And combined with the realities of the pandemic, it wasn't a good sight. Bellita might've been more ill than we thought.

While the doctor was examining Bellita, we prayed together and begged God to spare her with the hope it was just a terrible cold. I remember closing my eyes and opening them again to make sure this wasn't a dream. But once we were tired of praying, we sat in the waiting room with no intention of leaving. During that period, I applied to more jobs to kill time—even booking an interview. My parents called, but I was too busy reading job requirements I forgot to answer. Looking back, I was selfish, too absorbed in my little world to recognize what the reality was. Eventually, Clarisa got called to reception. And as she returned, she asked me a question.

"How come you still use the phone to work?" Clarisa asked with sadness in her eyes.

"No, but…it's just that we're sitting and waiting, and I figured I could use my time—"

"What is going on with you?" Hugo said. "Really, I do not understand. We work just like you, but value what's more important. It is family, *siempre. Canadá y México*. Tell your *jefes*."

Right then, *mis primos* looked at me with intensity. It seemed they had a million things they wanted to say yet couldn't find the perfect set of words to illustrate their disappointment. But knowing how much they hated my guts, I froze up. I didn't have the courage to explain my fallout with Milo, the depression I felt, and the hard time I was going through on a mental level.

Looking back on how I dealt with things, however, I wish I had been more honest and vulnerable with them. After all, Hugo wasn't condescending in his tone. He was just stressed out. Clarisa, in all fairness, brought up her point in a respectful way, despite her emotional state. Neither of them was picking a fight with me, yet their words still made me feel like a *pendejo*.

In the waiting room, I kept questioning why this genuine shame came over me with a strong presence. Was it because I felt out of place, lost, and with little direction? Or did I always feel a lack of belonging? I thought of how Milo and I were drawn to each other in the first place. Why did it hurt Milo so badly when he knew I didn't love him like he wanted me to? Either way, I couldn't figure it out. This eventually led me to do these journal entries. But after a long wait, three doctors emerged. They called us into their office. Suddenly, everyone's feelings toward me shifted to concern for Bellita—praying for the best. Hope was at the center of *mi familia's* mind.

When we all headed into the room, I noticed Diana texted me to let me know she was close. Diana had wanted to talk about something earlier that morning. I didn't know what, yet she also said it'd be too hard to do it over the phone or online. I texted her to meet me at the hospital, assuming she just wanted to see me for Valentine's Day. I knew *mi familia* wouldn't have liked Diana being around. But that was the problem: I didn't think. I was tired and stressed about Bellita, about being unexpectedly pushed back into the job market. I needed to be with Diana more than ever because I thought she'd understand. In fact, Diana was the only person I had left.

The office carried a dark, haunting energy that coursed through my veins. The walls were painted beige, and it felt cramped even though it wasn't a small room and there weren't any windows. It gave you the impression that it wasn't a place for good news, but a private area to explain the absolute worst. I realized we had to brace ourselves for what the doctors had to share.

"She has a high-level case of COVID-19," one doctor said in Spanish, with sorrow and empathy. "We're going to try our best, but Bellita isn't doing so well. She can't taste, smell, and is struggling to breathe. Unfortunately, because of her pre-existing health conditions, Bellita is also suffering more than the average person her age. It is not over. But…we'll do what we can."

"What'll happen if she doesn't recover fast?" Clarisa asked, trying not to fall apart.

"Prepare for any outcome," one of the three doctors said after a long pause.

Everyone burst into tears almost at once. It left me speechless at the grim reality the doctors portrayed for us. Nothing about life seemed right. Nothing was fair or true to me anymore. But instantly, I realized my unemployment and my tough luck in relationships never mattered. All I cared about was Bellita overcoming her ailment. I wanted to see El Castillo de Chapultepec with her, to show how much I loved her, how much

I needed her to be strong. In my mind, there was just no way Bellita wouldn't beat the virus. I'd never forgive myself if the worst happened.

"Can we see our Bellita now?" Jose asked once he regained his composure.

"Yes, I want to see her, too," Manuel said, wiping the tears from his cheeks.

"It is not possible," one doctor said. "You're very likely to get sick if you're in the same room for too long. It can be dangerous. We can't have that, unfortunately, because we're already overwhelmed. Maybe you can see her outside the room for a while. But… that is all we can do."

"I'll take my chances, *de la chingada*," Manuel said with fire in his eyes.

"Nobody cares!" Sara said, backing up Manuel. "We'll get sick, it's fine with us."

The doctors shared a look for milliseconds that felt like an entire lifetime.

"Come with me," one doctor said, following another long pause. "I'll bring you to her."

Staring at Bellita in her room minutes later, everyone's face painted with worry. She was lifeless from a distance on her bed, almost passed out. That's when reality struck me hard: Bellita wasn't in the greatest state as she fought with all she had to stay in this world. It was then Jose gathered us all together. We continued to look at Bellita, trying to get her attention. Hugo, Sara, and Manuel called her name and tapped on the window of the room's door to see if Bellita would respond. I remember feeling defeated, questioning why God made Bellita sick and not me? When Diana got to the hospital, I hoped she'd tell me everything was okay. I needed her love.

"Come," Jose said, stretching his arms. "Let us ask for forgiveness and good luck."

Suddenly, my phone vibrated. But I chose to ignore it.

"Dear father, the graces, *y todo la familia en el otro lado del universo*," Jose said with conviction. "If anyone must go to visit you, please make it be one of us. Bellita, our Bellita, has too much life to live for. She has too much she needs to achieve. It will break the hearts of many if she leaves us all behind. Please make her strong. Give her more time. Be there for her, *Dios*..."

Jose continued to go on until he brought himself to more tears. I almost followed his lead. Everyone was desperate for one thing: the nightmare of Bellita's situation to end. So much so that Hugo and Sara called up their bosses—letting them know everything, requesting immediate time off. Jose and Manuel were talking about who'd cover for them at *la taqueria*. Clarisa left to ask her main supervisor to revolve her work schedule around Bellita. But I read a text from Diana that indicated she was outside the hospital lobby. I pretended to take a call and rushed out.

Since Diana had COVID-19, I had kept in constant touch. I called and messaged her online, making sure my *Playa Crush* knew I was by her side. Even though Diana only took a few days to recover, I kept checking up over the last weeks. But from the moment Joie Media fired me leading to that February afternoon, there was a shift in our relationship. It seemed as though Diana viewed me as a different person. Better yet, it was apparent by the way she answered my texts, the way she responded to questions over the phone, and how she avoided hanging out with me since our day at *La Condesa*. And there was even a strange energy in the air when I spotted Diana at the hospital. She looked blankly in my direction. A hard conversation was coming up.

"How long have you in *Mexico*?" Diana asked, staring at me like she dreaded this.

"Two months," I said, reaching for her hand before she pulled it away. "But I want to—"

"I know you don't work for Milo now, so what is the plan?" Diana asked with intention.

For a minute, I couldn't speak. I felt Diana's eyes pierce through me without effort.

"Well... like I said before, I got two months left on my tourist visa. It's okay, though—"

"Sorry, *pero no*... I don't get how you will afford to be here for that much longer."

"I'm staying until March," I said, desperate to make my case. "And then, I'll take a bus to Belize and renew my visa there. I hear people do that a lot, so yeah. See, it's going to be okay."

"We are a dream, but not for good anymore," Diana said, while tears streamed down her face. "*Creo que... antes, si*, it was nice to talk and be at the same places. But how you pay to stay in Mexico if you're not with Milo? How long you have until you go forever? Who knows?"

"I'll get work soon," I said, beginning to feel Diana's pain. "This month... *te prometo*."

"But I have real doubts," Diana said. "You also need to understand... I leave to Miami tonight. Diego invited me and I like him. He also say the *pandemia* is not there and that is great."

"Diego from Cancun?" I said, feeling my heart slowly break into little pieces.

"Yes," Diana said matter of factly. "He and other friends will be in Miami."

I fell silent again. It was a pause that illustrated more than words could express. But at that moment, it occurred to me that Bellita and *mis primos* were right. Strangely, it even felt like Bellita was floating over my shoulder—comforting me as everything sunk in. It all made sense now "why" Diana wasn't as responsive to me anymore. My Playa Crush was beginning to fade.

"If you have a way toward Miami and have money and work, come with us," Diana continued, as I struggled to remain calm. "But it's not very cheap in Miami. You need stability."

Looking back, my Playa Crush was saying goodbye. Diana knew I'd never be able to join them on their trip but gave me the option to be nice. It was textbook fake-politeness and it cut deep. But despite all that I recognize now, I wasn't ready to give up who I loved without a fight.

"I'll figure things out really soon," I said, feeling discouraged. "And I'll see you in Miami, I-I promise you that. Please… don't leave me. Not now, and not like this. I just need more time."

"But I don't have," Diana said, looking at her phone. "I take Uber now… but see you in Miami if you're true to the words you say. I need to finish packing my bags. Sorry, I am going."

Even though I wanted to make a stronger case for Diana to stay, she already made her decision. All I could do was watch my Playa Crush vanish into Mexico City—exiting my life.

"If I meet you in Miami, will things ever be the same?" I heard myself asking Diana before she entered her Uber ride. "What I mean is… is it going to be like Playa, Bacalar, and Cancun?"

"Como que?" Diana asked, confused. "What you think we do so great in those places?"

"We traveled all over Mexico together for months, we worked together, we laughed and took photos," I said, trying to win back Diana's heart. "You introduced me to people, helped me open up to the world and… we'll always have New Year's. We shared memories together I'll—"

"No quiero un novio," Diana said, cutting me off before I got carried away. "I never do, and do not believe I will for long time. With the *pandemia*… I can work, take photos, see many different places, and all without anyone. I want good friends. That is it and all. You should, too."

"Please, don't do this to me now… I'll change because what I love most is you."

For a second, Diana turned my way with a smile that lit me up inside. Deep down, maybe she loved me back. Maybe I won her over again? I believed she would cancel her Uber ride and kiss me right there. But instead, Diana left me with a last piece of wisdom only she could deliver.

"Love is a moment you receive, it is not of people," Diana said. "That is what you must think of each time you have feelings. You love experiences. You love the food. You love the company. And if you are brave, you can have love for many others. So, you will have these feelings again if it is for here or in Miami. Remember us now, and you will find it more quickly."

"But what if I can't do it?" I said, about to cry. "You're so unique to me, I can't imagine—"

"Everyone with a soul is unique," Diana said. "But first, look within yours to know why you are special. That is what people see if you are true. My hope is… you find this love about you."

When Diana entered her Uber and drove off, I found myself close to a meltdown. She left me with good questions: should I work and travel at the same time? Create a life for myself full of enjoyment? Go visit her in Miami? Should I love myself? I saw the digital nomad trends online yet didn't consider being part of that culture and movement. I opened the hospital door with thoughts about that "chapter". But as I walked back in, *mi familia* headed toward the exit.

"Did the doctors say anything?" I asked them once we made eye contact.

Suddenly, I noticed there was a pain they were struggling to hide. I got a bad feeling in the pit of my stomach. I felt myself breaking yet didn't know why. And then, Clarisa fell to her knees—crying a storm of tears. Everyone looked just as sad. I didn't know what was happening.

"One hour ago…Bellita gone to see her *abuela*," Manuel said, looking pale as a ghost.

"Wait… what do you?... b-but wasn't Bellita stable?" I asked, trembling inside.

"No, she is not here!" Jose said, consoling Clarisa on the floor. "She with *abuela* now."

"How?" I said, instantly in tears. "But… she was alive before I went downstairs."

Right at that moment, I blacked out. It was hard for me to believe I spent Bellita's final hour pleading with Diana. Why didn't I focus on what was most important? I didn't want to tell *mi familia* what kind of conversation I was having minutes earlier. Honestly, I didn't want to accept Bellita was gone just like that. It appeared I was going into denial—convincing myself that Bellita and I would play a game of Connect Four later that night. I couldn't imagine a world that didn't include Bellita within it. That reality didn't make any sense. I felt more lost than ever.

"It was God's will," Clarisa said after she got back on her feet. "Before, she would have fought. But the covid was too much. We all knew Bellita miss *abuela*. And now... they are both together. I hope for *abuela* and Bellita to be safe. I hope they look at us and smile. I am in such pain, but at least... at least I know where Bellita is now. I hope she know that she was so loved."

Chapter 18

March 27, 2022

For the last month, I experienced a recurring dream I still can't explain. I saw Bellita feeding animals in a jungle. But she looked normal—healthy, strong, and cheerful. She wasn't in pain. She was the most beautiful thing I ever saw in my life. Before too long, I followed Bellita as she exited the jungle and ventured into a castle, where Abuela Velasco was accompanied by her husband. They kissed Bellita and gave her *dulces*. Most notably of all, though, Bellita's parents soon entered the castle with baskets of strawberries, apples, oranges, and bell peppers. Bellita lit up and embraced them with a hug. I felt as though I was an honored guest—a person from the living world, given the chance to report back my findings to *la familia* for their own comfort. Bellita looked at peace. It was a tranquility I felt down to my core, knowing love surrounded her. Maybe this was a sign from the universe. But it's something that made me depressed. It reminded me Bellita wasn't coming back. I woke up crying, my heart filled with endless regret.

I wanted to believe Bellita had more time. In my mind, she was dancing to salsa, lighting up the room with her talent. I wanted to believe she was going to beat me in Connect Four after dinner. I wanted to believe nothing other than the greatest things. But in the last month and a half, I became an isolated hermit, backpacking through Mexico trying to get over everything that happened. I didn't work, barely slept, and spent a lot of time drinking and partying in hostels. I couldn't imagine a world that didn't include Bellita in it. And since I had a month left on my Mexican tourist card, I figured it was best to ignore reality for as long as possible. It was a denial I held onto ever since mid-February. But it's also a deep hurt I thought I'd carry with me forever.

Currently, I find myself sitting alone inside the Italian Café I grew to love in Playa Del Carmen. It's one of the places I visited most when first arriving with Milo and my former team. But instead of socializing with others, I kept to myself in the back corner, away from the digital nomads surrounding me, trying to make sense of my thoughts, my dreams, and my future. Milo used to say journaling every morning was the "nectar that fuelled his soul for the challenges ahead." But so far, I have gained little perspective. I was avoiding reality, while I also tried to find my place in it again. Life moved on while I remained stagnant—watching travelers meet up with each other before going to the beach, talk about *cenotes* and the short bus ride to Tulum, and others tapping away on their laptops. Escaping the pandemic didn't feel romantic anymore.

Aside from Casa Velasco and my sister Gabriella, nobody else knew what I was doing. Guilt and shame had overloaded my emotions since Bellita's passing. The flaws in my lifestyle, the lack of my work-life balance, and the toxic nature of the culture Milo created for me at Joie Media became apparent only when it was too late. Suddenly, I hated myself. But what's more, is I hated the idea of a "career" and the fact companies expected you to sacrifice your life for the betterment of an organization that would happily replace you in a week. It happened to me, as I saw Joie Media posts announcing new hires like they did with me a year ago. It sucked to view it on my feed, yet I also prayed for those people, understanding they were in for one hell of a ride.

My parents had offered to fly me home to Montreal at one point this month. But I stopped answering them for weeks since I was just too depressed. They didn't know Milo had fired me. I kept isolating myself from those who loved me, especially when they'd reach out. But I only had a short time left in Mexico to get my shit together before anyone noticed the truth of me and Joie Media. I knew that I couldn't live off the grid in Playa forever. I recognized I'd have to face the music. My options were beginning to dry up. After all, my life savings could only take me so far.

That morning, I was tempted to get myself a bus ticket to Bacalar. I needed to clear my head, to escape the constant upbeat nature of Playa Del Carmen. But right as I was about to purchase my bus ticket, I got a video call request from Jose and Clarisa. It came out of nowhere. In fact, I haven't talked to them a whole lot for over a month. The fear of what they may say caused me to ignore their call. But when they called me again, I knew it must've been important.

"Hola, Max! We hear you are in *Playa o Tulum,"* Jose said with a serious expression.

"Yeah... I'm in *Playa,"* I replied. "Don't worry, though, everything is fine *conmigo."*

"It doesn't seem true," Jose said. "But that's not my point. How long you stay in Playa?"

"Guess we'll see for now," I said, unsure after a long pause. "I don't know exactly—"

"Please, come back to us," Clarisa said, looking as though she wasn't going to tolerate my bullshit. "We miss Bellita more than any person, but *somos fuerte.* I still go to work, I go see friends, and I laugh and sing. You need to be living on, moving forward, because it is the way to honor our *familia. Mirame...* you can't stop life because you are sad. Bellita would not like this."

For a minute, I had to force tears to stay at bay—away from onlookers in the café. Jose and Clarisa noticed my emotional state and waited for my response with patience. They knew my heart needed time to process their words and concern. It was evident I wasn't the only hot mess.

"Maybe, but... I just can't live with the decisions I've made, the person I was before, you know... all I want is to talk to Bellita, to feel her energy, and yet it sucks that I never will again."

"This is why tonight is so important," Clarisa said in a soothing tone. "It is hard to talk with you now, so we could not inform you of this, but tonight we have a party to honor the lives of Bellita and Abuela. Read your email, we already send you a flight to Mexico City. Come and enjoy *la fiesta* with us. Your mother and father will be arriving soon to *la casa*, so it'll be great."

"Yes, we invite Bellita's *amigos* from her salsa class, our staff *en la taquería*, the market*, y Abuela's* friends," Jose said, struggling to contain himself. "Everyone know that Bellita loved you very much, so it is necessary that you come. Your flight *es por la tarde*, so better hurry up."

"Thanks, but I don't know if I'm ready yet," I said. "It took me a lot just to walk to—"

"Nobody blame you for what happen to Bellita, believe us." Jose cut me off with a fire in his eyes. "It was *Dios*, and we accept. We miss you, dearly, and your parents also. The night won't be the same if you're not here. Bellita needs you there. We know she'll be there in good spirit."

After the video call ended, I saw Jose and Clarisa booked me a flight for 2:30 p.m. It was almost 9:30 a.m. by then, which gave me barely enough time to make it to Mexico City. But right before I got up, I saw the Italian Café's owner bring a group of four sweet almond croissants. Until this day, I can't explain why it teleported me back to the moment when Bellita opened up about her *panaderia* dreams. It made me laugh, thinking of all the sweet things she would've made. Suddenly, I felt as though Bellita was hugging me from the afterlife, letting me know she'd accompany me on my trip back. On the walk to my hostel, I remember talking quietly to her. And even though I didn't get a single response, it appeared Bellita was trying to communicate. It was a good feeling that struck my heart. And it followed me as I packed my suitcase, took the next ferry to Cozumel, made it to the airport, and eventually to Casa Velasco.

When I arrived, the outside of the house was decorated with Christmas lights, balloons, and *pinatas*. I stopped counting the number of guests after thirty. Everyone was smiling, salsa music played, some people danced, and of course, all Bellita's favorite treats were laid out in the dining room table. It was amazing to see all the people Bellita touched. I was also happy when Hugo, Sara, and Manuel greeted me with a shot of tequila. The energy was so hectic, I didn't have a chance to put my suitcase away. Then I spotted my parents, and knew I wasn't going anywhere.

They were with Jose, Clarisa, and a few other adults, laughing, clinking their glasses, and having a good time. The fact my parents came to Mexico City just to be at Bellita and Abuela Velasco's party said a lot about their characters. It was the most genuine thing I've seen them do.

Even though my parents didn't see me with all the guests surrounding them, I realized it was best if I made the first move. I couldn't run away from them as I did with everything else in my life. And I got this strange feeling Bellita agreed with that thought. Slowly, I walked up to them.

"Funny seeing you guys here," I said, while my parents lit up with surprise.

"You arrived!" Jose said, placing his hand on my shoulders. "Man, I see it is too difficult to find you now these days, no? What have you done? How is Playa? You enjoy it, *esperamos*?"

"We had our worries before," Clarisa said. "So, we are glad to know you arrive safely."

Smelling their breath, it was obvious they were drunk. It didn't bother me, yet my parents were uncomfortable at the party since they didn't consume alcohol often. They only came for Bellita and Abuela. Looking back on it now, they would've left early if they didn't see my face.

"You know… everything is good with me," I said. "It feels good to be with *familia*."

"*Orale!*" Jose said, as someone in the group handed me a beer. "May us cheers for *Bellita, Abuela, y toda la familia en el otro lado*. Let us not be sad now, but to celebrate their legacies."

After roughly twenty minutes passed, my parents wanted to speak to me privately in the guest room upstairs. It was a moment to be dreaded, yet one that was inevitable. I remember pulling my suitcase with me, thinking I'd place it in Bellita's old room since nobody else was using it at the time. But once the guest room door shut behind me, my parents were all business.

"What have you been doing the last few months?" my mother asked. "I've checked all the blogs on Milo's Joie Media and haven't seen your name anywhere. Please explain that to us."

"No, I...sometimes, editors become copywriters and copywriters become editors," I replied, shaking as though I was cold in the middle of winter. "That's the nature of the industry I'm—"

"Does that mean you're editing?" my father asked. "Listen, *Maxito*, we're concerned. We haven't been able to reach you and... and we almost thought for a second you were kidnapped."

"How did that idea even cross your mind?" I said, taken aback.

"But what did you want us to believe?" my mother said, her voice trembling. "Do you know how difficult it is not to think of the worst? It seems like you made a conscious effort to avoid us, so what did you expect? You're lucky your sister told us you've been active on social media, or else we would've launched an investigation! And now Jose and Clarisa are telling us that you've gone off traveling around Mexico. So... what have you been doing? It's obviously not work."

"I have been working... in fact, I've worked too much. More than I should have." I tried not to break down. "And it ended up costing me a lot of shit I didn't realize until it was too late."

"I'm sorry, but we don't know what that means... is everything okay with Milo?" my father asked. "You boys have been close since high school, so if you're having problems, just go talk to him. Fights are normal in any relationship. Sometimes, you are much stronger because of them."

"I don't know about that these days... and I really doubt you'd understand," I said, as my parents looked at me confused. I froze up for a second. I didn't have the ability to speak if my life depended on it. That's when my father uttered six words that felt like six blows to the groin.

"But I thought Milo loved you?" he said. "Again, you just need to communicate."

Struggling to keep it together, the truth had to come out. It was strange crying in front of my parents as a grown man. But that's when it hit me: I wasn't depressed because of my unemployment, Bellita's passing, or some greater lack of hope. No, it was because I never let the people who loved me love me back. For as long as I can remember, I pushed my family away to be accepted by a company, by Milo's well-respected brand, by a perfect "happily ever after" with Diana that was never meant to happen. But by keeping my sexuality to myself, I never gave my parents a chance to fully understand me. They never knew that complicated part of my life.

Despite this profound realization, however, I wasn't sure how my parents would react. Honestly, I've never been so vulnerable and embarrassed. But if I didn't confront my deepest fears then, I knew I'd risk damaging my relationship with them for good. That couldn't happen.

"Answer your mother, please!" my father said, pressing me more. "What is going on with you? Why are you behaving like this? Why aren't you talking with Milo? Is everything okay?"

"Yes or no?" my mother said, backing up my father. "Please, just be transparent with—"

"I'm gay...w-well, it's hard to explain," I said, unable to stop my tears. "For a long time, Milo had a crush on me. And I liked him, too, but it was just... I also like girls, and it was confusing to go through when I was younger...and that's what happened. I fell in love with this girl, Diana, at his company, and when I told Milo, he found a reason to fire me around the time Bellita got sick and... I'm just a hot mess now. I want to escape yet can't find myself in reality."

For a moment, my parents remained speechless. It was a lot to take in out of nowhere.

"Wait, does that mean you're bisexual?" my mother asked, hoping to give me a hug based on her body language. Her sympathy was present. It was an uncomfortable feeling at first.

"Yeah, I...I am. But it's more complicated than that," I said, after a long pause. "I'm drawn a lot more to the qualities I see in people rather than their looks, or gender, or whatever, and

I was stupid enough to fall in love with the wrong girl at the wrong time. I was crazy enough to think it could actually work…and right now, I got nobody and Bellita is gone. I just don't know what to do with myself… It's why I'm escaping. And it just feels like nothing will get better."

"That's how I fell in love with your mom," my father said, tearing up. "It was her soul, not her looks that made me understand I wanted her in my life. You have your old man's heart."

Nobody spoke. But I became happier for some reason. I felt my parents taking in the new information with absolute grace. Suddenly, my mother gave me a hug and my father joined in shortly after. We cried together. It was the greatest sense of relief I've ever had. The weight I carried with me since Bellita's death vanished, now replaced by love. In fact, the energy was so peaceful that I forgot there was a party happening downstairs. I forgot my world was a disaster.

"You know, I've always been proud of you since the day you were born," my father said. "And that will never, *ever*, change, *hijo*. I'm telling you now, my pride has only grown stronger."

"I love you no matter what," my mother said. "And I'm sorry you went through so much. I'm sorry you felt like you were alone. All we wanted to do was help, and I'm glad we can now."

"Me, too." I wiped my tears away. "I wanted to tell you guys, honestly, but… I don't know, it was just so hard… I didn't think you'd like me as much if I dated only boys and not girls."

Right then, my parents hugged me again. Their compassion enveloped me, and at that moment, I realized those old high school ideas were never real. I was no longer misunderstood.

"Hopefully, it won't take another twenty-five years to have moments like this again," my father said. "And I…I really hope now you can trust us with anything that you're going through."

"That's fair, I guess," I said, laughing a little bit. "I know it more than ever now."

"So, what's your plan?" my mother asked, a true smile gracing her face. "All we want is for you to be fine, so please give us peace of mind. It's my job as a mother to make sure of this."

"I'm going to find work again," I said with newfound meaning. "And...I promise it won't take me very long. Maybe I've isolated myself from reality, but I swear I'll get back on my feet."

"We'll give you a minute to relax before you rejoin the party," my father said after my parents released me from their arms. "But again, just know we're proud of you. Remember that."

For several minutes after they left, I laid down on the guest room bed and smiled realizing I finally had the guts to tell my parents everything there was to know that was in my soul. It seemed that a beautiful new chapter was about to unfold in my life. It prompted me to apply to jobs on my phone, thinking it would make this new beginning even happier. I went as far as reaching out to my former Joie Media team online, asking them how work was going for them, for career advice, and if they knew of any openings. One of my ex-colleagues replied quickly, said the team missed having me on board, and sent over a bunch of links to marketing agencies and media outlets that were in "desperate need" of a copywriter. By the time I left the guest room, I was on a roll, ready to jump into the market, to work hard, and seize reality again.

Before heading down to the party, though, a weird feeling came over me that I haven't experienced since that night passed. I still don't know how to explain it. But I had this strong urge to check if Bellita's room was still empty. I wanted to check on my suitcase, and sleep on an inflatable mattress or something after the party ended. I didn't want to share with my parents.

I was drawn to Bellita's front door like I was about to step into Narnia or an undiscovered world. It was the most powerful intuition I ever felt. Strangely, it appeared like Bellita's spirit guided mine until I was able to see her bed, her dresser, the Connect Four box, and all her old things. I remember sitting on my suitcase, texting on my phone, and refreshing my LinkedIn to see if more of my ex-colleagues replied to my messages. But looking toward Bellita's dresser, I noticed something that made everything inside me freeze up with emotion. It was the notebook I brought to her when I first got to Casa Velasco. And it was faced down on the table as though Bellita had written inside it every night since it was returned to her. My heart ached with pain.

Something encouraged me to read whatever passage was already laid out on the table. Looking back on things now, I was scared to find out what Bellita wanted me to understand. I wasn't the best cousin on earth, that was a given. But I also knew I could no longer speak to her anymore. Reading Bellita's thoughts and feelings might have been my last chance to be in touch with her. So, I picked up the notebook with trembling hands. I had to be brave at that moment. Mostly, though, I had to be strong enough to process Bellita's words and her beautiful insight.

"October 17, 2021:

I love, love, love, that I see Maxito, but I am sad he go. I know he works, but I want to see him more. I don't see him for a very long, long time and I don't like that he go after dinner time. Manuel say at la taqueria Maxito write things for a famous person. But I don't know who is?

I think Maxito can be famous if he try because he is nice and people will like that. I hope everything is okay in Canada with la familia, however, because I miss mi tia de Canada. I hope Maxito say her that my English is better than before. I have so much to say, and I know mi familia Canadiense will be proud. I hope forever that next Christmas we can be together again."

Tears quickly rushed to the border of my eyelids when I read "next Christmas" knowing it would never come. But there was something about Bellita's writing style that was moving. It wasn't perfect, yet it was full of charm and the natural ability to connect. I continued reading.

"December 31, 2021:

Tonight is a fiesta and it is fun, but I wish for Maxito to be here with everyone. I hope 2022 we can eat and dance. I don't hear where he is but think of him. I want to call Maxito very much, but mis primos say he is busy and will call for me later. Maxito will because he loves me.

I cannot write a lot tonight because I hear the salsa music, but I will pray for Maxito to be enjoying too. I believe 2022 is going to be so amazing. Cannot wait to share him my dreams."

Remembering what I was doing that New Year's Eve, I couldn't forgive myself for the way I behaved. Why did I spend all my time and energy on Diana? Why did I neglect my phone that night in Bacalar, thinking I was with my *Playa Crush* when that was never the case? It seemed like I was a different person, somebody delusional and toxic who didn't know any better.

"January 11, 2022:

I am happy for Maxito being at home, but I don't see him very much because of work. I see Hugo and Sara, but never him. He likes the door close at his room. I like to knock, but I am fearful he will not be happy with me. Work is important to Maxito, I see it more than before. I will try to work hard, so Jose will be proud of me because of Maxito. I hope he will be proud too.

Maybe I ask at dinner time if he is not working this weekend. I can ask when we play Connect Four because that is when we meet. I want him to come to dance with me at class. I know he would enjoy very much. Everyone knows about him, so they will make him so welcome."

Bizarrely, I smiled, knowing I had at least one great day with Bellita before she passed. I was proud I stood up to Milo and Joie Media—sacrificing a hectic workload for a moment with Bellita at *Parque Mexico*. I was happy she told me about her *panaderia* dreams, and that now I could have them with me everywhere I go. The only thing I regretted was not having more time.

I went on to read Bellita's words for what seemed like hours. Sometimes, Bellita expressed true hints of joy for the little things in life—from seeing people she loved at *la taqueria*, dancing to her favorite songs, and family members. But there was also the pain she expressed when *abuela* died. She kept writing "I want to see her in heaven" over and over. Bellita needed comfort, yet I never gave that to her. It hit me especially when I found Bellita's last passage.

"February 12, 2022:

I do not feel well, but I know it do not last for eternity. Jose say I am brave, and so do Clarisa. I miss seeing Maxito, and I know he is busy, but I want him to play with me. Maybe that help me be healthier. But I recall the day at La Condesa with Diana very well. I see Maxito has love in his heart and know he has love for me too. He is not like everyone in mi familia. Maxito loves so much that he likes boys and girls. That is a bigger heart than mine. That's why he works hard. I was sad before, but now I forgive him since he loves so much without knowing sometimes.

But I still hope Maxito love me to join me for dancing if he continue to be here in Mexico. He should love other things, not just the working he likes to do. I talk to Hugo and Sara, and they agree. Maybe I have a fiesta for Maxito soon. I want him happy. It cannot be so happy in his room all the time. I hope Maxito understand this, and he change. I miss mi primo Canadiense."

Right on cue, one of Bellita's favorite salsa songs began to play downstairs. It was a track by Martin Enrique—*Bailar Hasta Mañana*. The music picked up quickly, and I heard everyone go crazy with excitement, their feet stomping to the music. It was as though Bellita knew I'd find her notebook and that I'd get to this passage when that salsa track would blast from the speakers.

Grasping that I was in Bellita's heart this whole time brought about a sudden peace inside of me, a kind of warmth I doubted could be experienced. I couldn't help but dance in Bellita's room by myself—allowing the song to guide my rhythm. She gave me permission to start fresh.

Through the good and the bad I faced, Bellita was the one person who always believed in me, cheered me on, embraced the imperfections that were a part of me, and loved me more despite them. She was with me when I fell in love with Diana, got into trouble with Milo, and even until the final moments of her life. But above everything else, Bellita was right: I couldn't work myself to death or give my heart to people who never deserved it. That's what got me to recognize Bellita supported me as I naively chased after my *Playa Crush*. It used to be a romantic term, a fantasy that demonstrated all that I wanted instead of what I had. But in retrospect, it showed me what I didn't need and what was truly vital. My reminder of that every day is now Bellita and the lessons she taught. I have to believe in the universe—or, in other words, I need to see Bellita as a guardian angel. Every time I need her, she'll never let me down.

I exited Bellita's room with a better sense of direction. And with a month left in Mexico, I was going to apply for work while also spending time with *mi familia*. There was going to be more balance in my routine. Dancing to salsa once I rejoined the party, I talked to my cousins, my parents, and drank mezcal with Abuela's old friends. I felt rejuvenated, knowing I'd be okay.

And I smiled, knowing I'd be forever connected with my real *Playa Crush*.

Epilogue

December 15, 2022

Nine months after returning to Montreal, my life became more promising. Even though I'll never get over the pain of Bellita's unexpected death, I've learned how to move forward with the knowledge we'd someday play Connect Four again. But before that happened, I had more growing to do. Recently, I started a new job at a marketing agency as a junior copywriter. It's not where I imagined myself to be, yet it's remote and my managers have been nothing but kind.

During that time, my relationship with my family also improved drastically ever since I told them I was bisexual earlier this year. Who knew open communication was so healthy and rewarding, despite how impossible it is to be vulnerable. In fact, giving in to those feelings and understanding my deep issues is a big reason why being home in Montreal has been positive.

But even in my happiness, an interesting post entered my newsfeed this morning. Something I couldn't ignore. It inspired me to write my first journal entry since leaving Mexico.

Global company layoffs in tech and other industries have been trending on social media for the last few months. Hundreds of people, unfortunately, lost their jobs in a similar way that I experienced. I felt awful for them. But a small part of me felt gratitude in my heart. No longer did bitterness and depression rule over my world. And that's when I got a surprising message.

"Max, *mi amigo*!" Diego wrote to me on Instagram. "Ughh. I am so very sorry for you. Diana is upset as well about everything. Come to *mi tienda* and I'll give you more free tequila."

From the moment I got back to Montreal in early April, I blocked Diana and everyone associated with Joie Media. I needed a clean slate, and it helped me focus on getting my shit together. I had no idea what was going on. Better yet, I forgot that I had Diego on Instagram.

"Sorry, I'm confused," I replied twenty minutes later. "Is everything okay with Diana?"

"Milo," Diego wrote immediately. "He fire many people from Joie Media just now."

After doing some research online, I found out everything. Milo's third album didn't do well in sales, and it hurt his image. Other talented DJs released albums within the same period and were beginning to gain more social media attention. In a company-wide meeting, I read Milo announced it was time to restructure—causing him to dissolve more than ninety percent of "Joie Media". He wanted to pivot into strictly creating TikTok content on his channel, while also brainstorming new song ideas for his fourth album. "Back to the basics", Milo proudly stated.

"Sorry you got fired," Diego wrote after I haven't responded in a while. "Please, do say when you'll be back in Cancun. I will give you tequila, hugs, girls, whatever you want for real."

"Are you still in Miami?" I asked, suddenly remembering my final chat with Diana.

"No, no, I was there for only a short while," Diego replied. "It was quite fun to be there, and Diana and I did try sleeping together, but our energy wasn't alive. I recall Diana say to me that she liked you but picked us in the end. But it's so weird to explain well... sometimes having what you crave in your head isn't enough for your reality. It's like the omens stop once life brings what you desire, and being comfortable like this is no way to live with excitement. The journey is what always matters. And mine with Diana is no longer. On to all of the future ones."

Diego and I continued talking until our conversation naturally died out. But in that hour or so, I imagined how I might've felt if I lost my job near the holidays. Maybe it was meant to happen this way for me to see the value of things. I'm convinced Bellita gave me that message.

About The Author

Ian Ostroff is an indie author, copywriter, and digital marketer hailing from Montreal, Canada. With a passion for storytelling, his writing engages readers with a unique coming-of-age style and relatable narrative voice. He has made a mark in the literary world with his debut novel, "Socially Talented: Glen's Memories," published on May 17, 2022. Garnering acclaim from both reviewers and avid readers, the novel showcases Ian's ability to tell a story that can connect with anyone.

Beyond his writing endeavors, Ian's professional background as a digital marketer and copywriter adds depth to his literary expertise. With a good understanding of effective communication and storytelling, he brings a distinct perspective to his writing projects.

When he's not immersed in writing his books, you can find Ian planning his next backpacking adventure, playing sports, or seeking inspiration at local Montreal cafés and terraces during the summer months.

Connect with Ian on his website, blog, TikTok, Goodreads, and Instagram to stay updated on his latest projects, writing tips, and glimpses into his creative process.

Made in the USA
Middletown, DE
30 September 2023

39574452R00099